P9-DWZ-375

HE SAID SHE SAID

Shannon Layne

EPIC
Press

Jesse & Savannah
He Said She Said: Book #3

Written by Shannon Layne

Published by EPIC Press™
PO Box 398166
Minneapolis, MN 55439

Printed in the United States of America.

Cover design and illustration by Candice Keimig
Edited by Marianna Baer

LIBRARY OF CONGRESS CATALOGING-IN-PUBLICATION DATA

Layne, Shannon.
Jesse & Savannah / Shannon Layne.
p. cm. — (He said, she said)
Summary: Savannah leaves small town in California to seek out adventure on the white sand beaches of Los Angeles and meets Jesse. The differences between them appear bigger as their passion for one another grows, making them question if the summer flames find a way to endure.
ISBN 978-1-68076-037-8 (hardcover)
1. Summer romance—Fiction. 2. Interpersonal relations—Fiction. 3. High school students—Fiction. 4. Young adult fiction. I. Title.
[Fic]—dc23

2015932725

EPICPRESS.COM

For my Kait Kait,
who used to follow me everywhere.

"Promise me you'll always remember:
You're braver than you believe, and stronger than
you seem, and smarter than you think."
– A.A. Milne, *Winnie the Pooh*

savannah

When I was fourteen I was surfing off the coast of Moonstone Beach in Trinidad, California, a wetsuit protecting me from the chill of the deep water. I was a good surfer, but cautious, fearful of the power of the waves and what lay below them. As I lay flat on my surfboard trying to catch the next swell, I turned to see an eye as big as a dinner plate. Instantly, I froze, following the lines of the great gray body with my eyes. It extended into the water farther than I could see. The eye was barely a foot from me, and the whale just floated there, staring at me, as if it were trying to ask me what I was. Before I could think about it, I slid off my board and dove.

The water was dark and so salty and cold that even with my eyes open I could barely distinguish the whale from the water. He was so close to the surface that I almost ran into him. I ran my hands over his rough skin, over the barnacles and seaweed that made a home on his great body. I felt him begin to swim away, and as he flicked his tail to dive, I was caught in the backwash. Already underwater, I spun around and around in the eddy his dive created. I flailed and kicked but I had no concept of where the surface was. I couldn't find the light. As the last bit of oxygen in my chest evaporated, I caught a glimpse of the sun through the turbulent waters. I swam and swam, finding it much more difficult to reach the surface than it had been to leave it. Finally, I broke the surface. Heaving, battling waves, I climbed back onto my surfboard and lay facedown, coughing saltwater. The whale's tail had pulled me down nearly twenty feet further than I'd had to go to meet him. But from the moment I caught my breath and marveled again at what a whale's skin felt like under my hands, I was never afraid of the ocean again.

jesse

I grew up thinking there were groups of people that gathered around my house to take pictures because my mother was so beautiful. I never considered at age four or five that my family was somehow special because of it. In fact, I found myself thinking more often than not that it seemed like a giant pain in the ass that we had to go through life this way. They were like giant bees to me, the paparazzi and photographers that buzzed around my mother and father and me. It made it difficult for us to do anything without causing a scene. And my mother is beautiful, incredibly so—even as a child I recognized it. She had all this red hair that I was always trying to touch. It was thick and shiny and waved down her back, while her bright blue eyes were like individual topaz stones.

I rarely saw her. I was with a nanny or my dad most of the time. He wore glasses and could answer any question on Jeopardy! before any of the contestants. He taught me to catch a ball, to ride a bike. He was busy a lot of the time, too—he was a film engineer and was always off on set somewhere, but I saw him more than my mother. We were sitting at the kitchen table at our house in Los Angeles and I remember we had been playing catch and the leather of the glove was still stuck to my hand from the summer heat. My dad tugged on the brim of my ball cap and sat back in his chair, sighing. This was toward the end of everything, although I didn't know it at the time. I remember he looked tired.

"Dad?" I remember asking. "Dad, are you okay?"

He seemed to jolt in his chair, but he smiled and said he was fine, that everything was fine. It was the first time in my life that I knew an adult was lying to me.

Now, whenever someone mentions to me how

beautiful my mother is, what runs through my mind is something my dad said to me that day, when I found him staring off into space.

"Your mother never met a man she couldn't get her way with," my father told me. "One look, and you'd be willing to follow her to the ends of the earth." It was praise at the time, but after the divorce it sounded more like a warning.

CHAPTER 1
savannah

It's not until we're flying down the freeway in my friend Paige's truck that I believe I'm really going. I've been working toward this trip, saving up and planning, for months. But I never really thought that it would happen. I tilt my head back, riding shotgun as we fly so fast past redwoods and rivers that all I see is a blur of green and blue.

I stayed at home after high school graduation, working and going to community college. I can still remember the day I knew that I wanted something more from my life. I was sitting on my surfboard one Saturday, shivering a little and staring up at the gray sky, when it occurred to me that I was miserable. I was in the same place I'd always been my whole life, the same little town on the northern coast of California that no one had ever heard of.

For a moment, I began to imagine being stuck in this small town for the rest of my life. I pictured myself as one of those women I passed in the grocery store from time to time. The ones who looked like they used to surf, but hadn't been out in the ocean for months, or years. Too far removed from being able to remember what it felt like to be alive. This thought lingered, and shot a chill up my spine. I remember fidgeting on my board, trying to physically shake these thoughts away, but failing.

As I watched two seagulls soar and call to each other on the beach in front of me, I flung my wet hair away from my face and wondered, *Who am I?*

In that moment, I didn't know what I needed, or where I had to go; all I knew was that I needed something more. I wanted to go someplace where no one knew my name; I wanted to stand out. I wanted to be somebody in a way that just wasn't possible in a town of ten thousand.

"Itchy feet," said my mother. "Your daddy has them, too."

Looking at my dad, sprawled on our red couch with his feet on our yellow Labrador, Gus, made it hard to believe. But I knew that he had traveled the world in his twenties, after college, until he came back here and married my mom. Even Dad had gotten out. Even he had done *something*.

I didn't have the money to spend on that kind of trip, but I wanted to lose myself in unknown places like he did. I wanted to surround myself with people: bright lights and movie stars and new faces—I wanted to do it all. But I was content with starting small. Luckily, two of my best friends were in the same position and it wasn't hard to convince them to come with me. Sophie made it all possible, really. Her older brother lived in Los Angeles and had a friend who rents out a tiny beach house.

"It's, like, a three-room house, guys," said Sophie. "Seriously, it's tiny. But it's right on the beach."

"Right on the beach? Are you kidding me? Tell

him we'll take it," I said. "It's the best deal we're going to find by far."

"Holy shit, guys," said Paige, springing up from Sophie's bed where we were all sitting. She ran her hands through her short, blonde hair. "We're really going."

"We're going," I said, grinning. "I've been saving my money for months. We're fucking going."

A few weeks later, I hugged my mom and dad, kissed Gus, and hopped into the truck. My surfboards are in the back with my bags, and my backpack is sitting in the seat next to me. I already have a bikini on even though we won't hit LA for about thirteen hours. It's the middle of June, and as we head south I look around and mentally snapshot the world I'm leaving behind. I love where I come from—the redwoods, the beaches, and rivers. I grew up running barefoot through these forests. I spotted salmon and steelhead in the rivers and whales in the raging gray sea. Nowhere will be home the way this place is. But I'm looking for a new kind of paradise. Maybe a new me, too.

A shiver runs through my whole body, and I lean over and turn up the music that Paige already has blasting. I'm too energized to sit quietly in the passenger's seat. I want to feel the wind on my face. I want to say goodbye to everything I know in the best way I know how. I roll down my window and let the wind thrash my long hair into a wild mess as I unhook my seatbelt.

"Well, here she goes," says Sophie from the backseat. She's so used to my antics that nothing fazes her anymore. Paige, on the other hand, can always be counted on to freak out.

"Goddammit, Savannah!" she reaches an arm toward me, snagging my leg, but it's too late as I pull myself out of the window and perch on the edge. The wind brings streams of tears to my face. I fling an arm out and tilt my head back. Tree branches and sky blur into a mass of blue and green and brown and I reach out even though I know I'm not close enough to touch.

"Savannah! Get back in the car!"

"My legs are still in," I call through the window, and I hear Sophie start to laugh.

I sigh, breathing in the crispness of the air and then slide back into the car.

"You look like a lion," says Sophie, reaching from behind to ruffle my curls. My hair is almost down to my waist, and it's so thick that most of the time I just tie it up or French braid it. I shake it out around my face and lean back in my seat. I'm going. I'm really going.

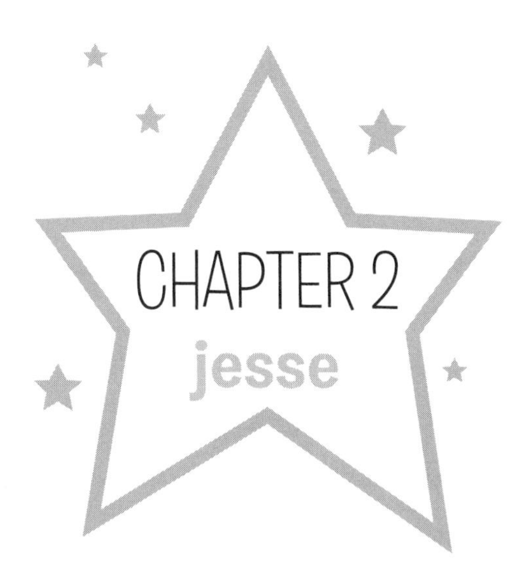

"Sir? Sir, we're about to descend. I can take your glass if you're finished."

I nod at her without looking, raising my seat back upright. I have a raging headache—most likely something to do with the several international flights I've taken in the past three days. I have never been so happy to be landing in Los Angeles. I run my hands through my hair and cross an ankle over my knee. My agent, Jeremy, is sprawled on the seat next to me, still snoring. There is plenty of space in the private plane but Jeremy always seems to end up in my personal space.

"Jeremy." I shake his knee and he jolts awake.

"Are we in Australia?"

"No, Jeremy, we're in LA. Remember? They changed the location."

"Right, right. Of course."

Jeremy doesn't travel well, but he is one of the most organized people I've ever met in my life. He sits up, instantly awake, and smooths his suit jacket as he turns on his iPhone.

"We're cleared to head straight to the house. The press conference won't be until tomorrow."

I nod, my eyes turned toward the window as I watch us approach the asphalt runway. I'm glad to hear Jeremy's update. I don't think I could handle anything but heading home, not tonight. The sun is almost below the horizon, and I stretch my legs forward and settle back into the leather seat.

Security blocks the way as Jeremy and I descend from the plane. A small group of reporters and paparazzi are there, shoving microphones in my direction and shouting questions. I'm a little surprised to see them, but there has been a lot of press generated for the movie I have coming out. I try to see it as a good thing and not another annoyance I have to wade through just to get home.

"Mr. Sharpe, is it true that you and supermodel Lila Swanson were seen together on the beach in Sydney?"

"Have you and Ms. Swanson parted ways? Are you seeing Elena Jacobs?"

I can't help but grin at the Lila Swanson question. It's true that we met up in Australia, although I don't think we spent much time at the beach. Security leads me through the crowd with ease, and I slide into the car provided just off the runway. Jeremy gets in next to me; the door slams and we're off.

"The changes have been made to the house, sir," says Jeremy. "The new floors have been installed, and the porch repaired."

"Sounds good," I sigh as I turn on my phone. The flood of emails from the director of the movie, my agent back in New York, and all the others flow in. I listen to the pings of my phone and I can feel my headache pound in my temples.

"Cancel everything tonight," I say quietly.

"Everything?"

"Everything, Jeremy. If I have to talk to one more person who is not you tonight, I'm flipping out."

"Yes, sir."

I built my house in Newport Beach just last year. It's all blues and grays, high ceilings, sleek and modern. I have art hanging everywhere—landscapes, mostly. I'm not much of an art aficionado, that's more my mother's area of expertise. I drop my bag in the master bedroom and clasp my hands behind my head. The wall facing the beach is entirely glass, leading out to a tiered balcony. I step outside and lean on the railing, breathing in the salty air. The beach below me is dotted with people, couples walking together or chasing after their kids. My dad is supposed to be here sometime next week; my mom said she'd be in the area, too, for some event. I stare down at the people below me, completely on my own for the first time in days, just as I wanted, but it doesn't make me feel anything but . . . alone. Frustrated,

I turn back to the master bedroom and the empty bed and decide to call it a night. I shut the door to the balcony and the drapes on the windows, closing out the sounds of the people on the sand below me.

"Wow, you were being serious when you said it was small."

The three of us are standing in the entryway of our new house. Looking in, I can see a sliding glass door that leads directly onto the beach. The living room and kitchen are connected in an open design, and both are tiny.

"How many bedrooms?" I ask.

"He said two," says Sophie, heading inside. Paige and I follow her into the tiny bedroom. One is a little bigger than the other. Luckily, there are two bathrooms.

"Let Savannah have her own room," says Sophie.

"She's going to get up early to surf, anyway. And she snores."

"I do not!"

I drop my bag on the floor and flop onto the mattress. Everything is bare; the mattress doesn't even have sheets yet. I pop up and start jumping on the bed, working out the kinks of sitting in a car for half a day straight. Sophie and Paige leap on and suddenly we're all screaming, bouncing up and down. I start laughing and spin in a circle, almost falling off the bed.

"We're here, guys!" I say. "We are actually here."

"And tomorrow we go out and look for jobs," says Paige, the responsible one.

"Right," says Sophie. "I just want a little part-time, easy waitressing job so I can sit on the beach most of the time. At least until my savings run out."

"Ditto," I say, jumping back off the bed. I have enough saved up to get me by for a few months, but a job would definitely make things easier. I open the tiny window and lean outside. I can smell the ocean and hear the hush of the waves on the sand, and it makes me feel at home. Sophie and Paige head into the kitchen to see if by some miracle there is anything edible remaining from the previous tenants. I lay back and link my hands behind my head, already making a list of everything I need. Curtains, sheets, food. Brownie mix, peanut butter, string cheese—the essentials. I hear Sophie squeal as she opens a cupboard, and I head into the kitchen.

"Whadja find?" I swipe a finger of the peanut butter they found in a cupboard and head outside through the sliding glass door. There is a tiny wooden landing and then it's just sand leading all the way to the ocean. I toss my shoes back in through the door and head outside. The wind is summer-warm, but the chill of the ocean breeze makes me shiver. I walk all the way to where the waves lap at the sand, letting the foam cover my toes and retreat. I turn and face our house, taking a look at what's just become my new home.

My view has changed from redwoods and mountains to billboards and more people crowded into one place than I've ever seen. Headlights create a stream of distant brightness from the freeway as I walk toward the water, taking it all in. There is so much energy, so much going on even at this time of night. I wade into the water; it's way warmer than the ocean at home, and much calmer. When a wave hits my thighs I stop and yank my tank top off before I dive into the dark water. I pop up and hear Sophie and Paige's voices approaching. I dive again, down to the sand at the bottom. It's too dark to see anything, but I run my hands over the bottom anyway, turning over every handful of sand in my fingers, like all the answers I'm searching for might be hidden somewhere at the bottom of the sea.

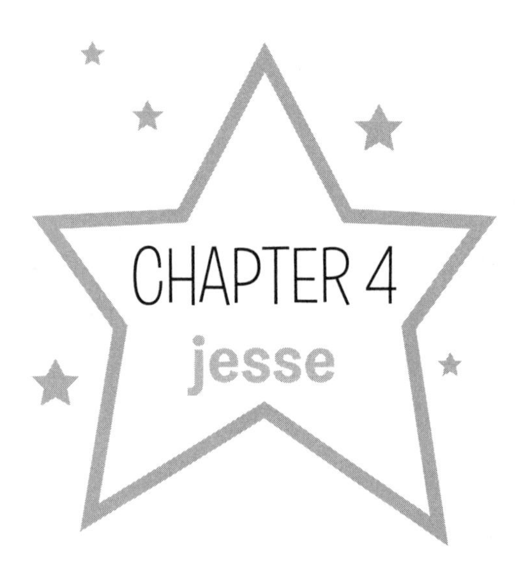

I'm sitting on my short board, way past the breakers, watching dawn come up in the east. I've been out here for twenty minutes already, but the regular surfers are just starting to show up. I haven't been surfing in so long that I had to dig my board out of storage. Still, I've spent plenty of time on the beaches of LA and I learned to surf when I was pretty young. I've never been too serious about it, but when I can, I still go out and enjoy the water. The casting director for the movie is standing on the beach, scouting extras for a few scenes, and I'm keeping an eye out while still enjoying the morning. I have a beard still, from the last film I was in, and I think that's helping people *not* recognize me.

I hear high-pitched chatter and roll my eyes. Sounds like a bunch of loud, obnoxious girls decided to come out and learn to surf today. I am surprised they're here so early, though. Turning my head, I can see that I'm right: there's one with short blonde hair, one with black, and one with the brightest blonde hair I've ever seen. They sit next to each other on their boards, laughing and teasing each other—at least, that's what I'm gathering. They probably don't even know how to surf, I think, shaking my head. The lifeguards are going to get called out in about a minute to save one of them. Just as the thought crosses my mind, the one with the long blonde hair stands up on her board. As I watch, small waves roll under her board and she balances easily before diving into the water. Out of the corner of my eye, I wait for her to pop back up, but she doesn't. Her friends are still just sitting on their boards, talking as the seconds pass.

I turn back around, watching other surfers. I'm sure she'll be fine. I have no idea who any of them are anyway, so what do I care? Against my own will,

I turn around again and curse under my breath. She's still nowhere to be seen, and it's been like a minute. Even if I don't know any of these girls, I can't watch someone drown while I sit ten feet away.

"Hey!" I yell, waving at her friends, who are still sitting on their boards. I'm just far enough for them not to hear me, and they're too busy talking to notice I'm waving. I scan the area where she went under but she still hasn't surfaced. I don't stop to think any longer. I undo the Velcro surf board leash from my ankle and dive.

The water is salty and green, stinging my eyes, and I dive deeper. I see a cloud of hair just below me and I snag her arm and start kicking toward the top. I feel her tug away from me and suddenly we both explode to the surface.

"What the hell are you doing?" she says, heaving for breath.

"You were under for a long time," I say defensively. "I thought you needed help."

"Well, I don't," she says, swimming back over to her board. I grab mine where it's drifted closer to the girls and haul myself back up, feeling like an idiot. Well, fuck, she must be part dolphin because I've never seen someone hold their breath that long.

"Who's your friend?" I hear one of the girls ask, and she just rolls her eyes.

"Incoming," says the other girl, paddling toward a wave. I see the girl I pulled from the water start to paddle before glancing toward her ankle and cursing. She sits up and straddles her board, reaching to re-attach her tether and glares at me.

"You made me miss that wave," she says.

"You didn't paddle fast enough."

"If you hadn't pulled me out, I wouldn't have wasted time yelling at you."

"I told you, I was only trying to help. I won't make that mistake again."

She sighs, turning her board toward me.

"I'm sorry," she says.

"Excuse me?"

She wrinkles her nose at me, and I notice she has a sprinkle of freckles across her face.

"I'm sorry," she repeats. "I snapped at you and you were just trying to help."

I'm trying to listen, but I'm also staring at her curves in her green bikini. She's got another sprinkle of freckles at the top of her thigh that I can't stop staring at.

"Apology accepted," I say, a little belatedly. "Can you make it back to shore?"

"Jesus," she mutters, tossing her wet hair over her shoulder. "Just when I was starting to like you."

She sizes up an incoming wave and starts to paddle with long, smooth strokes. As I watch, she pops to her feet and takes the wave like she was born with a surfboard under her feet. I look to the right and realize both of her friends are riding a wave nearly to shore, and I can't help but be a little impressed. I did not have these girls pegged as competent surfers; the one I pulled from the water might even be better than me. I paddle into a wave and jump to my feet, riding it nearly to shore before jumping off and wading through the breakers. The casting director, Mike Hamilton, comes right up to me.

We've worked on several other movie sets together in the past.

"Jesse, who were the girls you were talking to in the water?"

"I don't know. I only spoke to one of them."

"I want them for extras."

I sigh, running a hand through my wet hair. A woman walks by with her board and does a double take at my face, and I know we'd better act fast.

"They're the best surfers I've seen all day," he continues, "and we need pretty girls."

"I'll go talk to them, Mike," I say. "Alright? I'll be right back."

I leave my board in the sand with him and head down the beach toward where the girls are standing in a group. Why it has to be them and not any of the other perfectly capable surfers, I don't know, but Mike takes his job very seriously and I trust his instincts. Plus, if I'm being honest with myself, I wouldn't turn down the opportunity to talk to the blonde a little more. She was snappy with me, and no one is like that with me these days. I liked it.

I walk up to the three girls, and one of them squeals as she gets a better look at my face.

"Holy fuck," she says, "you're Jesse Sharpe."

I smile.

"I won't bother introducing myself, then," I say, and the girls gasp when I don't deny who I am. The one I pulled from the water stands like a statue, staring at me.

"You don't look like yourself," she says, and then blushes.

"You're right, I don't," I say easily. "I haven't shaved in a while, and my hair was dyed for my last movie."

"Oh, yeah, in *Saving Grace*, you had blonde hair," says the dark-haired girl. "I remember."

I nod. "Well, ladies, since you all know my name, do you care to share yours?"

"Oh right. Sorry," says the girl with the black hair. "I'm Sophie."

"Paige," says the blonde with the short hair. And, finally, I turn to the girl from the water.

"Savannah," she says quietly. Her eyes connect

with mine and I can see hers are green, like sea glass. I tear my gaze from her and refocus.

"I have a proposition for all of you," I say. A crowd is gathering around us as more and more people recognize me, but an audience has never fazed me.

"How would you ladies like to be extras in a new movie we're filming here in LA?"

"Holy shit," breathes Paige. "You're not serious."

"We're not actresses," says Savannah, frowning.

"Yes, I know," I say. "But we need surfers as extras, and according to my casting director, you three fit the part perfectly."

For a second, all three girls just stare at me. Sophie's mouth has actually fallen open.

"Will we get paid?" asks Savannah.

I grin. "I'm happy to say you will," I answer. "Of course."

"How much?"

Paige elbows her in the ribs, but the question doesn't surprise me. In her position, I'd probably be curious as well.

"Honestly, I don't know," I say. "But if you'll let me introduce you to the casting director, I'm sure he can answer your questions much better than I can."

I wave Mike over and the girls immediately flock to him, clamoring like seagulls. As I step back, Savannah leaves the crowd and follows me. She stands in front of me and glances at the group of people around us. Some are taking pictures.

"Why are you doing this?" she asks.

"I'm not," I say honestly. "Mike was the one who wanted the three of you."

She nods, and looks a little relieved. She glances back up at me, waves of hair falling in her eyes.

"I guess this means I'll be seeing a lot of you," she says, tilting her head up at me. A slow smile spreads across my face.

"Yes," I answer. "I guess that's true."

"Just don't antagonize me anymore."

"I tried to save your life, not antagonize you."

"I'm not a girl who needs to be saved."

"No," I muse. "You certainly don't seem like the damsel in distress type."

She grins and turns back to her friends and Mike. I watch her go, following the sway of her hips with my eyes. This movie just got a whole lot more interesting.

I'm still not totally sure how I went from applying for a job at Starbucks to being cast in a movie. We're just extras, sure, but who cares? We're going to make more this summer being extras than we would at Starbucks, and we get to make it surfing. I'm still soaking in the news. Not to mention that a movie star tried unnecessarily to save my life. I've repeated the story to Paige and Sophie a thousand times.

"I can't believe he came after you," said Sophie. "You were just a stranger."

We're sitting on the worn couch in the living room. I have a hot mug of black tea in my hands, my favorite.

"Well, if I really thought someone was drowning, I'd come after them too," says Paige reasonably. "Anyone would."

"So romantic."

I roll my eyes, but I've replayed the scene in my head over and over. The tug on my arm, the look on his face as we both surfaced. I can't believe I didn't even realize who it was. I blame the saltwater in my eyes. His beard does make him look very different, too. I've seen him in movies, on billboards, but I didn't expect to see him in real life. Ever.

"Do you know anything about him?" Sophie says. "Google him."

Paige pulls her laptop out.

"Uh, his parents are divorced. Mom is famous, too. Dad wasn't. Raised mainly in Los Angeles but they had property all over the world . . . It says here he went to Cornell. He plays the piano, snowboards, and surfs. Well, obviously."

A part of me wants to act like I don't care, but I am leaning forward, inhaling the details of Jesse Sharpe's life.

"He's been in the spotlight since he was young, because of his mother," Paige continues. "He was in a couple movies as a kid, but nothing big. He started his own career when he was seventeen and started modeling for Calvin Klein."

"I remember those commercials," says Sophie. "He's only a few years older than us."

Paige is twenty-two. Sophie and I are both twenty. According to Wikipedia, Paige says, Jesse is twenty-four.

"Since then, he's modeled for a variety of labels, guest-starred on several TV shows, and been in movies," Paige finishes.

I zone out of the conversation, thinking about this morning. We were both in the water, after he tried to pull me up, and the sun was reflecting off the water and it made his eyes seem so blue. I can picture them now in my head: bright blue eyes, such a contrast against his dark hair. I hope he has to shave for this part because I want to see more of his face, but I stop myself in the same instant. He wasn't even the one who chose us as extras—that was the casting director. We probably won't see him that much.

"When did the director say we needed to be there tomorrow?"

"He said five in the morning. I thought he was joking, but he wants to get the morning light in some of the shots."

I silently approve. I would most likely be up then to surf anyway, so the time doesn't bother me.

"Are they going to put us in full makeup?" I ask suddenly, thinking out loud. "I mean, we're going to be surfing, so that seems silly."

"I have no idea," sighs Sophie. "I've never been in a movie before. I don't know the ropes."

"Well, I guess we'll see tomorrow." I jump off the couch, plunking my empty mug on the tiny coffee table. Well, at least this place came with furniture. "I'm going to shower and then do you guys want to run and find some stuff for the house and maybe get a pizza?" I ask.

"Sounds good," calls Paige as I turn the lock on the bathroom door. The shower is tiny, but I'm short enough to fit perfectly in the cramped space. I strip off my shorts and bikini and hang them up to dry on the towel rack before hopping in. As I scrub my hair with shampoo from the half-empty bottle that Sophie brought with her, my mind wanders to my morning on the beach. Everything happened so fast that it's still difficult to believe it was real. I remember the way he looked sitting on his surfboard, with the light from the water still playing in his eyes. He'd looked so serious, like he was actually worried about me when he didn't even know my name. Thinking about his intense gaze and the way his eyes drifted over my body makes me shiver even though he's nowhere near me. Not only is he gorgeous, but he tried to save my life. If that's not romantic, I don't know what is. I wash my face and can't help but think that this guy could open doors for me. I've never really wanted to be in movies, but it can't hurt to have someone like him on my side. He's been places I've never imagined; his entire life has been completely different than mine, and I love that. I want to learn more about him. I flip off the water and roll a towel onto my head, grabbing another to start drying myself off as I walk into my room to put clothes on. Paige sees me walk down the hallway and shrieks like a banshee.

"Savannah, for God's sake put some clothes on! We have neighbors, you know!"

Sophie is cackling on the couch. "Jeez, Paige, how many times will it take before you stop freaking out every single time Savannah gets naked?"

I chase Paige around the house, screaming with laughter, before finally agreeing to get dressed so we can get pizza.

The next morning I'm up before the sun, yanking my hair into a ponytail while I sit in bed. We have about a half hour before the car will be here to take us to the place where we're filming. Mike was in the middle of explaining to the three of us how to get there when Jesse interjected that he'd have a car pick us up. Nice of him, and probably smart. None of us are used to this area yet and I'd be willing to bet we'd get seriously lost if we had to get ourselves to the location. I fill a backpack with bikinis. At first I feel like an idiot for packing it, but I want to make sure we are prepared in case they expect us to bring our suits to the set. I tiptoe into the kitchen and make coffee in Paige's Keurig. Ever since I woke up, I've been edgy. I've never been the best at being patient. Sophie drags herself into the kitchen, grunting at me. She doesn't do mornings. I hand her the cup of coffee I brewed for her and she gulps it. Paige walks in briskly, already in her bikini, just as a horn sounds outside.

"Holy shit, it's happening," says Sophie, sprinting into the bathroom to brush her teeth. I pull my backpack on. It's stuffed with a sweatshirt and my water bottle. I have no idea what today will hold, but I'm ready to take it on. We all pile into the sleek backseat of the car and the driver turns to us.

"Welcome, ladies," he says pleasantly. "My name is Alan. I'll be your driver this morning. Some music or would you prefer quiet?"

"Music is great," I say when Sophie and Paige just stare at each other. "And thank you for picking us up."

"It's my pleasure, Miss . . . "

"Savannah," I say. "And this is Paige and Sophie."

"A pleasure. Now, ladies, sit back and I'll take you to your first day on set."

We drive for about a half hour to an isolated stretch of beach north of our little house. I don't pay much attention to the road and suddenly we end up in a parking lot and Alan instructs us to grab our bags. Someone is waiting at the edge of the parking lot where the asphalt meets the sand. A woman walks over as we pile out of the car and extends her hand.

"Welcome," she says. "I'm Jenna, one of the production assistants. If you'll follow me to the makeup tent we'll get everyone fixed up."

She is perfect despite the early hour, with a smooth ponytail and dark mascara, and I find myself trying to smooth back my hair, which is springing to life in the morning mist. She leads us onto the beach and into one of the trailers on the edge of the sand. We walk up the steps and my jaw drops; the whole trailer is crawling with people. I can see hair dryers, boxes of makeup, huge mirrors. How in the world do they fit all of this in here? Jenna leads us to a man with the most perfect eyebrows I've ever seen in my life and he immediately grabs me, pushes me into a chair, and starts brushing my hair. I see Sophie and Paige get yanked away by two other makeup artists and then my hair is flung in front of my face and I don't see anything at all.

"You have the perfect hair," says the man currently pulling a brush through my curls. "So thick and so long."

"Yeah," I say, "I've been meaning to cut it."

He turns my chair so I am facing him, his hand on his heart.

"It would be a sin against nature to cut this hair, darling," he says. "I must insist."

I can't help but smile up at him, and he extends the hand that isn't holding the brush toward me.

"My name is Antonio," he says with a thick accent.

"I'm Savannah."

"Oh, and such beautiful eyes as well. I hate to ask you to close them."

He tilts my head back as I smile and close my

eyes, he then starts brushing something over my eyelids.

"Why are we all getting made up if we're just going to be in the water?" I ask.

"There will be some shots with you three in the background that take place on the sand," says Antonio. "But you may not need full hair and makeup tomorrow. For now, there are certain things we are going to do that will highlight your natural beauty in the morning sun. A little contouring, some shimmer so your pretty eyes catch the light."

I just lean back and sigh as he starts brushing through my hair again. I am excited to hear that our gig seems to be longer than just one day.

As it turns out, filming a movie scene is a lot of standing around and doing the same thing over and over again. They place us on the beach with some other minor characters, telling us to stand this way or that, look right, look left. Finally, someone snaps "he's coming out of makeup now" into their Bluetooth earpiece, and he walks through the mist.

And holy shit, he looks hot. I didn't get the chance to appreciate him properly when I thought he was just some annoying guy. He's even better-looking in real life than in his movies, if that's possible—all that tousled dark hair, the intense blue eyes. He talks animatedly with one of the directors, and I watch him out of the corner of my eyes. Toned stomach, broad shoulders. Physically, this guy is just about perfect.

Jesse turns and sees the three of us standing on the edge of the sand and walks over to us.

"Good morning, ladies," he says. "Thanks for meeting so early."

Sophie yawns hugely, but I am more than awake.

"Sure," I say. "It's not every day we get asked to be in a movie."

He grins at me lazily with just one side of his mouth and I feel a slow twist of excitement in my stomach. One of the directors walks over to us and turns to Jesse.

"Jesse, if you're ready, we're going to go ahead and begin," he says. "Let's get the girls in the water."

"By all means," says Jesse, and Paige and Sophie immediately turn and head for the water, chatting to the prop master about the surfboards they're providing for us.

"I see makeup got to you," Jesse murmurs to me as I turn to go. I look back at him over my shoulder.

"Unfortunately," I say, and he laughs.

"You look lovely," he says quietly. "Your eyes look so green in this light." I know he is an actor who can deliver a line, but I can still feel my heart flip-flop in my chest. I'm surprised by his candor and the way it's making my pulse jump. I flash him a cocky smile to hide my discomfort, ignoring the flush I can feel spreading on my cheeks.

"You don't look so bad yourself," I say cheekily, and his eyes widen but he still gives me another half smile as I turn and head into the water.

The salty air and cool morning breeze clears my head, helps me refocus. The last thing I need is to develop some stupid crush on a celebrity who I'm going to see for as long as they need me as an extra and then never again. Luckily, it's much easier to concentrate on the water, as Sophie and Paige and I catch wave after wave for whatever scene it is they're trying to capture. Finally, they wave us in for a break. I catch a wave and ride it easily all the way to the breakers before jumping off in knee-deep water.

"These waves are so different," I say to Paige and Sophie as we head straight for the snack table. "And the water is so much warmer."

"It's a lot safer here, you know that," says Sophie, her mouth stuffed with an orange slice. "These LA city slickers would die so fast if they had to surf in our part of the Pacific."

I feel rather than see him behind me before I hear his voice.

"Are you talking down about us Southern Californians?" says Jesse, reaching around me for a handful of pretzels. "It can't be that different up north."

"Yes, it can," says Paige emphatically.

"Well, I'm ashamed to say I've never been in that

part of California," says Jesse. "Maybe one day you'll all have to take me."

He is such a flirt, but it's so hard to resist. Someone runs up to him suddenly, whispering in his ear.

"Excuse me," he says, and walks away, to take a call or something, I guess.

I turn back to the table for a cup of orange juice as a group of people crossing the parking lot catches my eye. One of them breaks out of the crowd and runs toward Jesse.

"Is that Lila Swanson?" Paige gasps. Out of the three of us, she is the only one addicted to celebrity news. I've watched her sit through eight hours of *Keeping Up With the Kardashians* without coming up for air.

"Who?" Sophie and I say at the same time.

Paige sighs. "She's a supermodel," she hisses. "An international supermodel."

Lila Swanson, international supermodel, shrieks and throws her arms around Jesse and I'm intensely annoyed for reasons I don't understand.

After another couple of hours, the director wraps the scene. The sun has started to pierce through what was left of the morning mist, and the light is much harsher.

"That's all we need you for today, girls," one of the directors says to us. "We'll let you know when to be on set tomorrow."

We turn to head back to the car and almost run directly into Jesse and his supermodel girlfriend. To my surprise, she smiles warmly at all of us and immediately extends a hand.

"I'm Lila," she says, shaking hands with all of us. "Jesse told me how he found you yesterday on the beach."

Sophie answers her and I just stare at her arm wrapped around Jesse's waist.

"I can't believe this is your first time in LA," says Lila. She has a thick accent—Australian, I think, but I'm not completely sure. "How funny you ran into Jesse."

Jesse smiles. "It was certainly lucky."

Lila gasps, clapping her hands together and leaning toward us.

"A few friends came with me from Sydney," she says, "and we're all getting together at Jesse's this evening. You must come."

We all start to protest at once. I feel almost obligated to say no. I'm not a supermodel. I'm not even an actress. I'm sure I'll feel out of place and awkward. Then I look at Lila and her huge smile, and the arm she's slung back around Jesse, and I hear myself say:

"Of course we'll be there. Just give us the address."

Jesse raises his eyebrows, and it looks like he's fighting a smile even as his brow furrows slightly. Lila squeals with excitement. Jesse waves his hand and his driver is suddenly at his side.

"Sir?"

"These three will need a ride to my place tonight. You can pick them up and take them whenever they choose to go."

"Yes, sir."

Well, that makes things easier. Jesse and Lila turn

to go and I watch his eyes glide over me and a strange expression crosses his face, almost like a wall, closing him off to me. I already have what feels like a thousand butterflies in my stomach doing the tango. I have no idea what tonight will hold. All I know is that I can't wait to see him again.

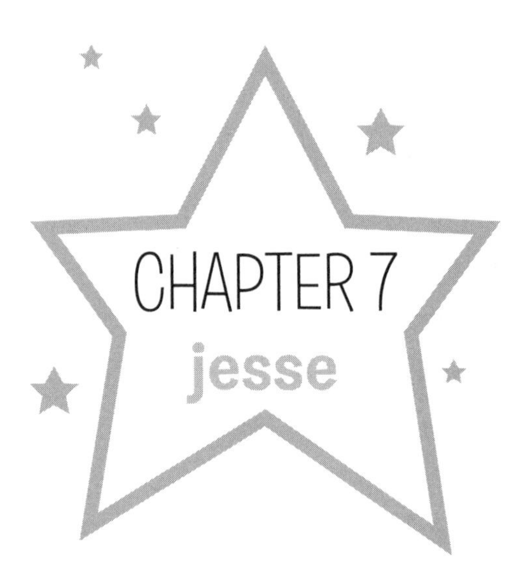

CHAPTER 7
jesse

“Of course I was going to invite them, Jesse,” says Lila. She is currently sprawled on the chaise lounge where the back patio meets the sand. Her perfect body is curved toward me and she’s topless.

“You could have at least run it by me, first,” I grumble. “I barely know them.”

Lila stretches arms toward the sky on the lounge and my will to argue with her fades from my mind.

“Let’s not fight,” she says, reading my hesitation perfectly. She sits up, pushing her sunglasses down so I can see her dark eyes as she hands me the bottle of tanning oil. She turns so her bare back is toward me and pulls her hair forward over her shoulder. I’m still not happy she invited Savannah and her friends to my house, but it's too late to back out now. The truth is, I would love for Savannah to come. I'm just not sure I want Lila there, too. And that in itself is a dangerous emotion to consider, period. I curse inwardly. I had no idea Lila would be in Los Angeles today, let alone that she would show up at my movie set. I haven't heard from her since I left Australia last week, but she has a photo shoot in the area and stopped by. I pop open the bottle of oil and pour it into my hands before rubbing it into her bronzed shoulders. She makes a sound of satisfaction and twists toward me, pushing her breasts into my slick hands and I decide to drop the subject.

A few hours later, the sun is setting over the ocean and the entire west side of my house is infused with the colors. I'm standing on the balcony outside the master bedroom, enjoying the light over the waves, when Lila comes up behind me. She wraps her arms around my waist, her cold hands digging into my hips.

"I love this shirt on you," she murmurs, slipping

her hands inside the white button-up that I pulled on after my shower. "Shows off your shoulders. And black jeans, too. You make quite the picture."

"So do you," I say. And she does look lovely, her long hair smoothed into waves and her curves encased in dark blue silk, but something about it comes off as cold to me. She leans up and kisses me, running her nails along my back. Lila dwarfs some of my shorter friends, but she has to reach up to kiss me. She pulls back, giving me a small smile, and twirls away.

"I'm going to check on the drinks," she calls. "Come down when you're ready."

I turn back toward the ocean and take a breath of the last moment of solitude I'll have all night. I'm strangely restless and on edge, and I wish I had the time to surf or go for a run to burn off the nervous energy. I need a drink. I button my shirt slowly, shoving my hands in my pockets as I finish, and turn to head inside. I walk through my bedroom, stepping over Lila's towel that she left on the floor, and take the stairs two at a time.

“Darling, where are your shoes,” scolds Lila as I enter.

“I don’t want to put them on yet.”

I beckon one of the housekeepers over and quietly instruct her to go into my bedroom and pick up Lila’s towel.

“I’ll take a whiskey on the rocks, Henry,” I say quietly to the bartender, and he immediately pours me a glass. Headlights flood the front windows with light.

“They’re here!” Lila calls, and the party begins.

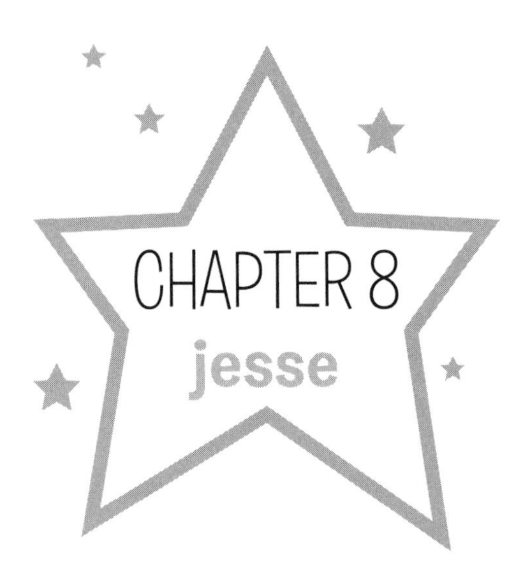

Within an hour, my house is packed with people. People involved with the movie as well as friends of the other actors and actresses involved have all come to drink my alcohol and make my head pound with the noise.

"Really, Jesse, it's good publicity," Jeremy says to me. "You have very important people here." I sigh and finish off another whiskey; instantly, a waiter takes my empty glass and replaces it with a fresh one. I nod and he disappears into the background again. Jeremy is engaged in talk with one of the set directors, but the music is blasting so loud it's difficult to hear what anyone is saying. I turn to head upstairs to my room for a breath of air when a flash of light catches my eye. She's here.

Savannah stands out in this crowd like a strip of gold in a tapestry of dull brown: her hair is wildly curled in a waterfall down her back, which her shimmery bronze dress leaves almost entirely bare. She is wearing gold stilettos to match, with straps that wind around her ankles in a way that makes my mouth water. She hasn't seen me yet as she walks in the door with Paige and Sophie. Her eyes scan the room and I swear I can see the flash of green all the way from here. Her dress hugs her body, highlighting her slim legs and the curve of her breasts. With a back like that, there's no way she's wearing a bra. I can feel my body jump to life and I have to take a minute to calm myself before I approach her. That dress tonight is going to be the death of me.

"Hello, ladies," I say smoothly, catching up with the trio at the door. They are standing together, laughing and talking animatedly, but Savannah sobers as I approach. Sophie and Paige give me wide smiles and immediately start thanking me again for the invitation, but Savannah hangs back and I can feel her eyes on me.

"This place is amazing," Sophie exclaims. "The windows, and the view of the beach. It's incredible."

"Thank you," I say. "I hope you all enjoy your evening here. Can I get you something to drink?"

Everyone nods, even though Savannah still hasn't said a word. As I catch her eye though, she gives me a smile that makes my nerves scream. There's a silent connection between us, and I know she feels it too. I don't know why, but having her close makes it hard for me to breathe. She walks past me with her friends to head to the bar, and as she does, she brushes against me, just barely touching my chest, and I want to drag her upstairs into bed. She glances back at me with a sideways slant of those green eyes, and as I meet her gaze her mouth drops open. I watch her order at the bar. A moment later, she grins and downs half a beer in one draft while her friends order fruity cocktails. Lila's favorite drink is a Cosmopolitan, but I can't bring myself to touch it.

As the night goes on and the alcohol flows,

everyone starts to loosen up. Shoes come off, jackets land on the floor, and I even catch sight of Lila's silver stilettos gracing one of my chairs. The whiskey is making my entire body buzz pleasantly. I'm having a conversation with one of the production managers about the movie when I notice Savannah and her friends. They're walking onto the outside patio where a DJ is blasting music and there's a crowd of people dancing.

"Excuse me, Dennis," I say. "Let's continue this conversation later—have Jeremy schedule you in," handing him off to Jeremy as I casually stroll outside. The music is loud and energetic and as I enter the crowd I can see I'm not the only one with my eyes turned toward the three girls. Savannah is still in her gold stilettos, a drink in one hand and Sophie's hand in the other, and her dress is sliding over her skin as she moves. It slips off one shoulder and I so badly want to step toward her and slide the rest off, let it pool at her feet.

She turns her head slightly as she dances, sees me standing in the crowd, watching her, and I see her cheeks flush. Everyone else is entranced by the music and the darkening night, and I can feel myself getting a little excited as Savannah subtly turns toward me. Locking her gaze with mine across the dance floor, she begins to move, twisting her hips and sliding her hands on her thighs. She doesn't take her eyes from mine. I'm frozen, locked in another world with her while everyone else disappears around us.

I've been with supermodels and professional athletes—I'm not trying to brag, it's just a fact—but none of them has ever come close to turning me on as much as I'm turned on right now. I can't keep my eyes off her body. She turns her back toward me and I watch where her waist curves. I want my hands there. I pass my drink to a waiter, stride over to Savannah, and take her hips in my hands, my front pressed to her back. She reaches up and runs her hand up my neck into my hair as she grinds on me with no hesitation, and I can't seem to stop my hands from running over her body. Paige and Sophie are too busy dancing themselves to pay too much attention to Savannah and me, and, for once in my life, I feel as though there are no eyes on me at all. It's just Savannah and I and the feeling of her skin, slick with sweat under my hands. I can smell her perfumed skin, musky and sweet at the same time, and I'm so wrapped up in her that I can't take it anymore.

"Come with me," I whisper in her ear. I take her hand and lead her through the crowd of drunken people, out of reach of the music and up the stairs. She follows me step for step until finally I pull her through my bedroom door, locking it behind me, and she takes my face in her hands. I press her back flush against the door, locking her hands in one of mine above her head, and I race kisses from her neck to her shoulders. She makes a purring noise deep in her throat and tilts her head back to allow me access to more of her skin, and I can't help but smile. There's no hesitation, no false modesty—she is pure sensation, pure need.

"Touch me," she whispers, and in one motion she pulls her dress off her shoulders and exposes her breasts to my hands.

"Savannah," I breathe. That was unexpected. And so fucking sexy. She is perfect, all silky skin and clear eyes that lock onto mine, and I step toward her and take her newly bared skin in my hands, flicking my thumbs over the peaks. I feel her shiver and sigh, and it's all I can do to keep myself in control. A warning bell is beginning to sound in my head. I really wish it would shut off, but it's growing louder. I allow myself a few more seconds of touching her perfect body, kissing the spot behind her ear and returning to caress her mouth with mine. Then I place my hands on either side of her head against the door so I am not touching her. We both pant as though we've just run a race.

Watching her chest rise and fall gives me another jolt of arousal. Fuck, this is impossible.

"Is everything okay?" whispers Savannah, and I glance up at her face to see wide, concerned eyes. Her dress is still hanging from her waist, but she reaches up to cup my jaw in her hand without seeming in any way self-conscious.

"Yes," I say. "Everything is fine. I just had to stop."

"Why?"

"Well, trust me, I didn't want to," I grumble. "But this isn't the right time."

"You're probably right," sighs Savannah, and I smile to hear the note of regret. "I know you're right, actually. I'm kind of buzzed anyway. And just being around you makes my head fuzzy." She licks her lips, which are swollen and puffy from our encounter, and I think I might explode.

"Don't do that," I whisper. "You are driving me crazy."

She just smiles, tilting her head pertly as her lips curve upward. All I can do is stare, mesmerized. She gathers her dress and covers herself again. I'm disappointed to watch much of her body disappear under the fabric, despite her revealing dress.

"So, what's going on with you and Lila?" she asks, and I detect genuine concern. "I know this is a little late to say, but I really like her. I'm not trying to fuck up your relationship."

I raise an eyebrow at her. "We don't really have a relationship."

Savannah looks at me dubiously.

"We have . . . relations," I say.

She rolls her eyes. "Figures."

I snort and she laughs, leaning down to adjust her shoe.

"I'm glad you stopped us," she says. "I think I would have, too, but it would have been later."

"Really?"

"Yes. But I would've been saying no, as in not now. Not no as in never."

I can't stop looking at her, with her flushed cheeks and messy hair. I wind my hands into it like I've been wanting to all night, tilting her head back so her eyes meet mine.

"You are something else," I say.

She smiles. "That's a compliment I've never heard before," she whispers. "Let's go back to the party. My friends will be wondering where I am."

"Do we have to?"

"This is your party," says Savannah. "And you don't even want to be here?"

"I get claustrophobic."

"Bullshit," she snickers.

I laugh. "You're right. I just have a headache. Even actors get tired of small talk after awhile."

"I believe that. I'm terrible at it. I just always say what's on my mind. It gets me in trouble."

With a start, I realize that I am having a normal conversation. No bullshit, no thinly veiled small talk about how much money I have or what it's like to live my life. I feel like I could just as easily be the pizza guy, and she wouldn't treat me any differently. It's so refreshing.

She turns, stroking my jaw again, and presses a kiss to my cheek. One minute we're inches away from tearing each other's clothes off, and the next we're having a normal conversation like we've known each other forever. It's unnerving. She turns from me, opens my door, and hops down the stairs as though she's walking on clouds and not four-inch heels. I close my bedroom door and resign myself to having to wait to touch her again. I run my hands through my hair, wishing I'd never taken my hands off of her, but at the same time, I'm glad I did. She is so tempting, but I need to get myself under control. We come down the stairs and re-enter the party; it's so loud and dark that I don't think anyone missed us. Just as the thought of control crosses my mind, Savannah turns and looks at me over her shoulder. As soon as our eyes lock, all coherent thoughts leave my mind all over again. She stops in her tracks, too, trapped by the power of our gazes on each other.

"Fuck," I say under my breath. This is going to be harder than I thought.

"You're lying," says Paige. Sophie is still comatose in her old striped bathrobe with the hood that she only pulls out when she's hung over.

"I'm not," I whisper. I stare right in her eyes so she knows I'm serious. "It was amazing."

"You barely know him."

"So what?"

"Be reasonable, 'Vannah," sighs Paige. "I just don't want you getting hurt."

"Please!" I scoff. "We've made out all of one time, and you're worried about me falling in love with him like some moron?"

"It happens."

"Not to me. I know what I'm doing."

Paige looks at me shrewdly, and then sighs. "If any of us could say that and mean it, it would be you. I've seen you break so many hearts at home."

Although it is strange hearing her talk about me like this, I know she is right. Still, I remind myself that I am in uncharted territory here. There have been guys I've fooled around with and never thought about again, but this is already starting to feel a little different. Of course, I would never admit that to Paige.

I chuck a pillow at her, and she doesn't bother to duck. We're all wrecks: my hair is pulled up into a messy bun and I'm in a loose sleeping tank top and panties. Paige is wearing a long-sleeved shirt that says "Bite Me" on the front. She has dark circles under her eyes and a bottle of water in her hand, and I know I can't look much better.

Sophie stumbles into the kitchen and straight to the Keurig.

"You doing okay, Soph?" I call.

Her response is nothing but a grunt.

"Savannah hooked up with Jesse Sharpe last night," calls Paige, and I hear the crash of a dropped mug.

"Here we go," I say, barely audibly.

"Excuse me?" Sophie pops her head out of the kitchen, her bathrobe slipping down one shoulder.

"Come in here," Paige yells.

Sophie comes in with a new mug full of coffee, plops next to me on the couch, and begins to slurp.

"What the hell happened?" she asks in between sips. "I don't remember anything past being on the dance floor with you guys."

"You were dancing with one of the other actors," I say. "Kyle, or something."

"Oh, right."

"We came home pretty soon after that," I say. I remember it so clearly despite the alcohol: the wind streaming through my hair in the car, the places on my skin that still felt as though they were burning even though he wasn't touching me anymore. I keep getting flashbacks of his eyes as he pulled away from me—they were so dark, so intense that my breath caught in my throat.

Sophie and Paige start discussing the previous night, and I sit silently. I try to follow along with them, but I'm gone. I'm lost in the world of last night, imagining his hands on me, pulling me toward him. He made me feel like he couldn't wait one more second to touch me, and I remember the pressure of his lips on mine.

I absently run my fingertips over my bottom lip, thinking of how his mouth felt while he was kissing my neck. Just thinking about it is getting me worked up all over again. It was an instant connection—something I've never felt before. I thought I'd die if he didn't touch me. I remember pulling my dress down, his hands on me, and I shift in my spot on the couch, pulling my other leg under me to sit Indian-style.

"You're crazy, Savannah," sighs Sophie. "But I'm jealous. He's hot."

"We're filming today, aren't we?" Paige interjects.

"Yeah," I say. "They pushed it back a little now that we're finished with the early morning shots, though. So we have time to shower before the car gets here."

"Thank God," moans Sophie as she heads toward the bathroom.

I stand up, stretch, and head to my room and tiny bathroom. By some miracle our hot water heater is big enough for both showers to be on at once, and I'll be quick.

When I get out, I am scrubbed clean all over, but I still feel branded. I rub my favorite peppermint lotion over my legs, but every time I touch my own skin, all I think of is him. I wonder what it will be like, seeing him today. I wonder if Lila will be there, and I feel a prickle of guilt before I remember that she was definitely dancing with another cast member. Obviously the two of them aren't anything serious. *Or is that just wishful thinking?* I wonder. I shake off my nerves and yank a sweatshirt over my head. It doesn't matter what I wear to set, since they just put me in a bikini as soon as I get there.

"Savannah! The car is here!"

I head toward the front door, trying to shake off my nerves. It's not that I'm nervous to see him again, exactly—it's just that ever since last night, my whole body feels like it's streaming with electricity. Everything looks sharper, somehow. I slide into the car next to Sophie and hope that surfing will work the edge off.

Antonio takes an extra ten minutes on my hair and makes me lie back with cucumbers on my eyes for the puffiness. Apparently that really works, because when I sit up again you would never know I'd been drinking until two in the morning. In fact, I look like I've been at a spa for three days.

No wonder movie stars always look so good.

"Holy shit, Antonio," I say. "You're a miracle worker."

"Don't let your hair get that tangled again," he sighs. "And don't drink so much. You are too young."

"True," I admit, and I leap up to kiss his cheek and then bolt out of the makeup trailer. They choose a bright pink suit for me today, with a ruffled top, from the arsenal of suits I brought from home.

I leave the wardrobe trailer and head toward where Sophie and Paige are already corralled on the shore. I'm fixing a tie on my suit as I walk through the sand, and I frown as the tie sticks.

I'm still messing with it when I slam into someone with so much force it lands me on my butt in the sand.

"Hey!" I say, shading my eyes to see who bumped into me. "Watch where you're going."

"I could say the same," a voice says wryly, and my stomach jumps into my throat.

"Oh," I say. "Hi, Jesse."

He extends a hand and there's clearly a jolt between our palms as he helps me out of the sand. His eyes are a perfectly clear, piercing blue, different than last night.

"How are you feeling?" he asks quietly, his eyes scanning me.

"I'm fine," I say. "I had a lot of water before bed."

"Good call," he says with a hint of a smile. He

holds my gaze for another minute, and my mouth goes dry. He reaches out and gently skims his thumb over my lower lip. I smile, thinking about last night, and his eyes soften.

"Don't look at me like that," he murmurs, and he walks toward the director with a backwards grin at me. I continue toward the edge of the sand on legs that are shakier than they were five minutes ago.

With the late start, morning passes quickly and suddenly it's time for lunch. I wade out of the water with Paige and Sophie. My hair is still dry—we haven't even had to surf yet today. The director just wanted us in the water in the background for a few shots. It seems silly to be getting paid to stand in the ocean, at least to me, but I'm not going to complain about it. It sure beats waitressing. I elbow Sophie out of the way so I can grab a sandwich and she half-heartedly slaps my arm.

"I'm starving," mutters Paige, shoving her way

in between us. She starts talking to another extra, a tall guy who surfs too.

I'm grabbing a napkin when I glance up from the table and see Jesse staring at me. Our gazes lock and my knees buckle and I am frozen. He just stands on the other side of the long table under the shade of a tent, but he has me in a spell. His blue eyes pierce through me, and reflexively I lick my dry lips.

His gaze goes dark and he turns toward his private trailer, glancing back at me, and even though my legs are shaking, I know I'm supposed to follow. I want to. I'm in love with this heady feeling, the absolute craziness of this attraction. I love the way my body responds to nothing but a look from him.

I skirt around the table, out of sight of the crowd. I edge my way around another trailer and dart up his steps and ease the door open. His trailer is cool inside and perfectly clean. It smells of him. I shut the door behind me. He has the biggest trailer, and the inside is nicer than our little house.

I catch a glimpse of a sleeping area and a spacious bathroom before he appears from the back. His eyes are blazing and he's changed into soft, faded jeans from his swim trunks. He still isn't wearing a shirt and his muscles ripple as he walks toward me.

"Hi," he whispers, snaking his arms around my waist and nibbling on my ear. I am an instant tangle of firing nerves. It feels so deliciously sneaky that almost no one knows.

"Hi," I say, my breathy voice giving me away. "My ears are ticklish."

He pulls away, smiling, and I take advantage by leaning in and laying kisses on his skin all the way up his neck to his jawline. He tilts his head forward, his jaw muscles tensing, and I kiss his cheek and then finally press my mouth to his with so much force he stumbles backward into a counter. He opens his lips and I caress his tongue with mine. He slides his hands up my back, tangling his fingers in my hair, and I whimper.

I am completely lost.

He tilts my head back, biting my lower lip gently. All that is blocking our two bodies is my bikini and his jeans. I can't resist sliding my hands over his bare skin. His muscles bunch under my hands as I lightly run my nails down his back and he groans and grabs my hips roughly.

"Savannah," he breathes, and I know what he is going to say and I'm not ready. So I press my body against his, wrapping my hands around his wrists, and he relents, meeting my lips with his again.

He spins me around, lifting me at the same time, and sets me on the granite counter. I run my hands through his hair as he kisses me, squeezing his hips with my thighs. I can see how aroused he is. The bulge in his jeans is obvious, and I feel a quiet thrill at what I can do to him.

He takes my face in his hands, pulling our lips apart, and we pause. I am breathing so hard, my chest rising and falling, and he tilts his forehead to mine. I close my eyes, listening to his breathing and trying to get mine under control.

"Jesus, Savannah," he says.

I smile and feel his answering grin against my lips. I link my hands behind his neck and pull him closer, wrapping my legs around his waist. He brushes his lips over mine, taking me under, and I breathe out slowly. I'm so wound up and so calm at the same time; I've never met someone with that effect on me before. I've never met someone with such a strong effect on me *ever*, actually.

"We should go back out there," he says. "We have another few hours of filming to do before we're done."

"Let's skip it."

"Excuse me?" His mouth quirks up as the words fly out.

I grin and ease forward, brushing my mouth against his until his tongue comes out to meet mine. He groans, moving his hands to my face.

"I guess you can't play hooky," I gasp as his teeth graze my neck. "Being so important and all."

"I am the lead actor," he says, his mouth still on my skin, and I tremble.

"Yeah, yeah," I tease, and he smiles at me. There is a second of quiet.

"Meet me tonight," I say.

The words are out of my mouth before I can stop

them. I've never been good at keeping my mouth shut or hiding something I'm feeling. And I want to see him tonight so badly it's making my entire body ache.

He stares at me, his eyes dark and intense. He cups my chin in one hand, his thumb skimming my lower lip.

"Are you sure that's a good idea?"

I know the consequence of the words before I say them. Being near him is dangerous; both of us admit that already. It's too intense. And despite my brave words to Paige this morning, I'm worried about what will happen to my heart if I get closer to him. It frightens and exhilarates me, the thought of spending more time with him. Right now, I'm not sure which emotion is stronger.

"No," is all I say in return, and he frowns.

"Does that mean you don't want to see me?"

"No."

His mouth quirks up in a smile and my heart spins cartwheels in my chest. He looks so young for a second, so different from his normally serious self.

"I know what you mean," he says, sobering. "I don't know if it's the best idea either."

"Because of Lila?"

"No," he scoffs. "Although I should level with her about things. She's leaving for another location tonight anyway."

"Are you sad?"

He gazes at me, his eyes still smoldering.

"No," he says quietly. "Let's go back out there. You first. Make sure no one sees you."

"Why do we have to keep this—whatever this is—a secret?"

"Full of questions today, aren't you?" he murmurs. "I'm not sure, honestly. I just don't want to mention it to anyone yet. I'd prefer if you didn't say anything either."

"I told Paige and Sophie," I say, and his eyes widen.

"Seriously?"

"They're my best friends," I say defensively,

rolling my eyes. Doesn't he know anything about girls? "I'm not going to apologize for that."

He grins at me. "Feisty little thing, aren't you?"

"I just don't like being told what to do."

"I can see that," he snorts, and I narrow my eyes at him as I hop off the counter.

He snags me by the waist, nuzzling my neck from behind as I try to squirm away.

"Mmm," he whispers in my ear. "I like it when you fight me." His hands snake down over my thighs and I yelp.

"Let me go," I say, half-heartedly trying to pull away from him.

"You don't mean that," he whispers in my ear, and my blood pressure spikes. But he releases me, planting a kiss on top of my head. "Let's go. We have work to do."

He hands me his iPhone, and I type in my cell number and the address of our house before turning to the door of his trailer. I open it slowly, glancing around, and then run down the stairs, opting for the most innocent expression I can manage.

Sneaking around is exciting. It adds a layer of thrill to everything. Maybe what he said about keeping us a secret wasn't such a bad idea.

We are surfing in the next few scenes while Jesse and the other lead, another famous actress whose name I can't recall, act out a scene on the beach. I'm sitting on my board, letting the waves roll underneath me as Jesse and the actress lay out on the sand. I can't see them very clearly with the light reflecting off the water and into my eyes, but I see the movement of his hand on her face and my hands clench on my board. In the same instant, I stop myself. What is wrong with me? Jesse isn't mine. He's a movie star with every capability of delivering a line. I should take everything he says with a grain of salt. I sigh, running my hands through my hair. This is exactly why I shouldn't get involved with Jesse. We're so different, and considering how little I actually know about him, I definitely shouldn't feel so attached already. But every time these thoughts run through my head, another part of me interrupts. I can never turn down a challenge, and that is exactly what Jesse is. He's complicated, spoiled, incredibly hot, and closed off in a way that is hard for me to understand.

I can't tell a lie to save my life—everything is on the surface. I'm just hoping no one actually asks me about Jesse and me or I'll blow our cover in a second. One of the production assistants waves at me from the beach, urging me closer to shore, and I flatten myself to my board to pick up a wave, pushing thoughts of Jesse from my mind.

"First you hook up with him at the party," says Sophie. "Then you sneak off with him while we're at lunch. And now he wants to meet tonight?"

"That about sums it up."

We are back home, sitting in the sun that comes through the living room windows. Paige just showered and her short hair is drying in a curtain around her face. She is sitting wrapped in a towel and watching me with narrowed eyes.

"I don't like this," she says.

I roll my eyes.

"Paige. We talked about this. I'm a big girl."

"You're still a girl," Paige says. "You have emotions and they're going to get involved."

"What's wrong with that?"

"What if he doesn't feel the same way?"

"So what if he doesn't? I haven't said I feel anything for him, anyway! Paige, seriously. You are such a mother hen."

"I'm just looking out for you."

Because I know it's true, I relent. "I know. But really, Paige, I can handle myself. Whatever happens between me and Jesse, I can handle it."

She crosses her arms, but sighs, and I know I've won. I jump off the floor and leap onto where she sits on the couch. She squeals as I wrap my arms around her.

"I love you," I whisper into her hair, and she hugs me back. Sophie crawls onto the couch too and adds herself to the sandwich.

"It'll be fine," says Sophie. "'Vannah's crazy, but she's not stupid."

"Thanks a bunch."

"I can't believe this is happening," says Paige.

"We're in Los Angeles for about fourteen hours and Savannah gets saved from the ocean by a movie star who then falls in love with her."

"He's not in love with me."

The thought gives me a twirl of panic in my stomach.

"Speaking of being in love," says Sophie, "Mike came up to me during filming today. I thought he was hitting on me, but apparently I just had seaweed in my hair. It was really embarrassing."

"That's random. Mike Hamilton? The guy who hired us?"

"Yup."

I snort, picturing the scene.

"I just wish he would give me a speaking role," Sophie sighs. "I think I was born to act."

"If you're saying you're a huge drama queen, then yes," says Paige.

Part of me is listening to their conversation, but my veins are thrumming with excitement. My mind is stuck on Jesse as it has been all day. I have no idea what is going to happen with Jesse and me, long-term or just tonight, but I love that. I love not knowing what is going to happen next. I run my hands through my hair. I hope he comes tonight. His house really isn't far from this little one. It occurs to me that I really don't know Jesse that well; in fact, I know close to nothing about him. What surprises me more is how much I want to know about him: What was he like as a child? Did he always want to act? A vision comes to mind of a little boy with Jesse's bright eyes and dark hair. He must have been a beautiful baby. My parents have baby pictures of me everywhere and I think seventy-five percent of them are blurry, and in the other twenty-five percent I look like some sort of jungle creature. I shake my head. Besides the fact that nearly everyone in the world knows Jesse's name and face, including myself, he is a stranger to me.

After another few hours in the living room with a bottle of cheap wine Paige picked up at the store down the street, my roommates head to bed. Sophie is still hung over and Paige has the sleeping habits of an eighty-year-old woman.

I can't stop pacing in my room. I check my phone, but there are no messages. Finally, I flop down on my bed. I'm wearing my favorite yoga pants and a loose white top with no bra—what I would normally consider wearing to bed. I'm not going to put on a good outfit and have him not come and waste it.

Just as I start to debate crawling under the covers and calling it a night, there is a knock on the back door. My heart freezes in my chest and then starts beating so loudly I'm sure he can hear it. All of a sudden, I am less sure of myself. A part of me wants to go out there and tell him that I can't do this, that we're different people, that it won't work. Because I know if I see him tonight, there's no going back. I won't be able to step away after this point as though nothing ever happened. Even as I wrestle with myself internally, I've known all along what the answer will be. I stand up, throw the covers off me, and walk to the door. He is standing in faded jeans and a dark hoodie, hands shoved in his pockets. His lips curve into a smile when he sees me. He looks so good standing there that I hesitate to slide the door open, but I do anyway.

“Hi,” I say softly.

“Hi,” he says, and he steps inside and wraps me in his arms. I lean into him and the battle that’s been raging inside my mind all day slides away.

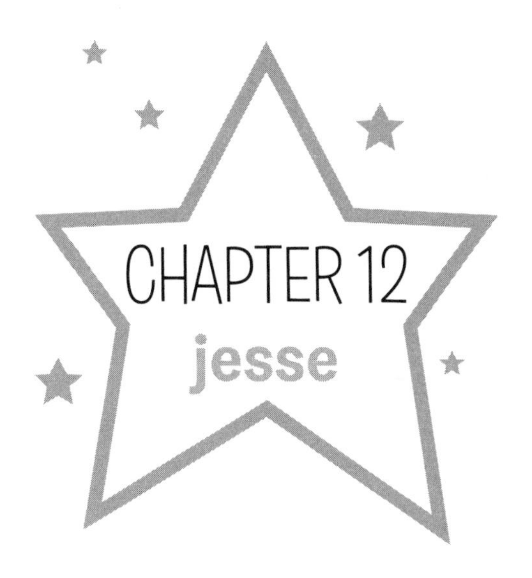

She smells so good, like peppermint and clean sheets. As I hug her, I realize I've missed her since I saw her last, and that's a new sensation. I don't know what this girl is doing to me. I tilt her chin up so I can see her face. Her hair falls down her back. She's wearing a loose shirt that slides off one of her shoulders.

"Can I come in?" I ask, and she steps backwards into the house.

"Sure," she shrugs. "If you want to."

I come in, sliding the door closed behind me. This house is tiny but homey. There are blankets thrown over what little furniture there is, and it's clean. There's a wind chime hanging near the back door made from shells and sea glass and as soon as I see it I know Savannah made it—probably brought it from home because there's no sea glass or shells on the beaches around here.

I walk around the living room, through the dining room, and past the tiny kitchen in about four steps. Then, I'm in the hallway.

"Is this your room?" I ask her, pointing to the door on the left. She has her fingers twisted in the hem of her shirt and it's adorable. I think she's nervous, but I have no idea why.

"Yeah," she says. "Right through the door."

"May I?"

"Again, if you want to." She shrugs.

I don't know why I'm curious about her space, but I am. I know so little about Savannah as it is, that everything I pick up is important. She's not someone who talks a lot about herself, so walking through her house is an opportunity to learn about her. I step through the door and instantly grin.

The room is tiny, barely big enough for the twin

bed, a dresser, and a nightstand. But the ceiling is strung with clear Christmas lights and the bed is covered in a soft blanket the color of the sky. There are pillows covering nearly every inch of the bed and the window is wide open, letting the night in. There are sweatshirts all over the floor, and I can see at least three bikinis hanging up on the towel racks in the attached bathroom. The entire room smells like peppermint—Savannah.

"What?" she says, breaking into my thoughts. Her arms are crossed.

"I like it," I say, and she relaxes.

"I didn't think this was really your style," she says. "You live in mansions and fly private jets."

I shrug. What can I do? Deny it?

"That's the life I'm used to," I say. "But that doesn't mean I can't appreciate a different style."

"Are you going to feed me all that bullshit now about how you're really just a normal person?"

I throw my head back and laugh as she loops her fingers through mine and leads me down the hallway. The truth is this conversation is not super comfortable for me. It reminds me of everything that has driven me away from having a serious relationship.

"How is Lila?" she asks, trying to sound nonchalant, but I hear the worry in her voice.

"She's fine," I say. "She's headed to another location to shoot a swimsuit commercial. Somewhere in the Bahamas, I think."

"Did you tell her about us?"

"I told her that I thought we should end our relationship." And that's the truth. She reacted exactly as I'd expected—calm and friendly. Our relationship was very superficial. She didn't have delusions about what it was. I want to tell Savannah that—without making myself look superficial, too—but instead, I get ready to field more questions.

"And she was fine with that?" Savannah sounds doubtful.

"Yeah," I say. "It was very simple, honestly."

Savannah is the exact opposite of Lila, I realize. And that means I have to learn about the life she leads in addition to her personality, because I'm honestly out of touch with what that's like. That's one of the things that attracts me to Savannah. She treats me like any normal guy, not like a celebrity. She's so normal that she's extraordinary. And I seem to find every detail of her life intoxicating.

"Walk on the beach with me." I mean for it to come out lightly, but she spins and looks at me as though I've just poured my heart at her feet. Her eyes search my face and I feel the connection build between us the way I am beginning to expect. I take her waist in my hands and kiss her once, twice, light and teasing. Her lips curve and I kiss her nose before I take her hand again. Her hands are tiny compared to mine.

"I almost expected you to have webbed fingers," I say as I lead her out the back door. "You can hold your breath for so long."

"I used to hold my breath in the bathtub when I was little," she says, smiling. "My parents panicked, too."

The moon is high in the sky above us and as we

walk through the cold sand, the waves flood over our toes.

"How do you do that?" I ask, genuinely curious.

"I don't know. I'd been working on it for so long that I think I just built up my lung capacity gradually."

The wind blows over us, cold air carried from the ocean.

"Are you cold?" I ask, and she shakes her head.

"Not at all. At home it's so much colder that everything here feels warm."

"Did you surf at home?"

"Oh, yeah. Always."

"Is it different?"

"Yeah. It's much colder, much more dangerous. There are sharks."

"Jesus."

She laughs. "But I love it. It's home. There's nothing like it."

"What made you come here?"

"Look who's full of questions tonight," she murmurs, looking up at me. I shrug, brushing it off as though it's not a big deal, but in reality I am dying to know these things about her. It's vaguely irritating, really. And distracting. I forgot my lines at least three times today because I was sneaking looks at Savannah in that little bikini in the ocean.

"I love home," she begins, "but I needed to get out. My dad had itchy feet like I do. I just want to go places, and do things, and not stay in the same place I grew up and where everyone knows my name. And there was nothing, no one, to keep me there."

Her cheeks are beginning to flush.

"I know what it's like to have everyone know your name," I say. "But you could run from it. I can't."

She nods slowly.

"You said there was no one to keep you there," I say.

"Yeah. I had a couple of boyfriends in high school, but nothing serious."

"Are you a virgin?"

She raises her eyebrows at me as a laugh bursts from her mouth, but she doesn't look embarrassed.

"No," she says levelly. "I'm not. Are you?"

"No," I say, grinning.

"Do you care that I'm not?"

"No." I frown. "Should I?"

"No. I wouldn't care if you did, anyway. But some guys don't like it."

"Some guys are morons."

"Most," she says pertly, sticking her tongue out at me.

I laugh, and we walk in silence for a moment.

"That's something we have in common," I say.

She smiles. "What, that we're both not virgins?"

"Not quite," I say wryly. "And my case is a little different than yours, but still. I know what it's like to have everyone know your name and want to run from it. I know what it's like to want more."

"That's exactly it," she says. "I wanted more. I needed it."

"I can understand that."

"You have everything," she says.

I shake my head. "No," I say. "Not even close."

I turn to her abruptly, taking her face in my hands, and she gasps as my tongue invades her mouth. I fight for control, tracing her cheekbones with my thumbs, the smudge of freckles across her nose that I find so fucking irresistible. I pick her up in my arms, swinging her legs over, and she reaches up to clutch my neck.

"Jess," she squeals, and the way the nickname just rolls off her tongue makes my whole body clench. Fuck, I think even the way she talks is sexy. I wade into the water, both of us fully clothed, and she screams so loudly I think my ears will fall off. She begins to shake in my arms, and at first I think she is mad, but then I realize she's laughing.

"Let me go," she screams, flailing in my arms, and I drop her in the water. She pops up, soaked from head to toe, her hair in a stream down her back. She just grins at me.

I stare at her, her hair shining in the moonlight. Her shirt clings to her skin and I can see the outline of every curve of her body. It is all I can do not to peel that shirt off of her, here, in the middle of a public beach.

I reach a hand out to her and pull her close to me, tilting my forehead down to hers. She is breathing hard. I can see goose bumps on her chilled, wet skin. I run my hands down the backs of her arms, and she looks up at me. We're standing about waist-deep in the waves, which are lapping against our bodies.

"What?" I ask, gripping her hips in my hands.

"You look good wet," she murmurs, and her words are all it takes. I wind my hands in her wet hair, brushing my lips over hers. I tug her hair gently so her chin tilts toward the sky and I kiss the line of her jaw and then press my lips to her neck. She is shivering now, but I don't think it's from the cold. I taste the salt from the water on her neck and slide my hands under the back of her shirt.

"Oh," she says, so quietly I think I imagined it. I am too busy running my hands along her bare skin to be sure. With every touch, she shudders as though every time I touch her it's an electric jolt.

She jumps up, wrapping her legs around my waist, and takes my face in her hands. At first it's almost too much for me, too personal to have her touch me that way, but then it feels so good I can't stop. Her mouth is hot compared to the chill of her skin. My hands run over her body, over her breasts and the thin, wet material covering them. I growl in frustration, wanting her bare skin. She gasps and moves her lips to my ear. I am hard, ready, but trying to be gentle. I kiss her neck, turning us away from the beach. With her facing me, I slide my hands beneath her clinging shirt and over her slick skin until her breasts are cupped in my hands. I brush my thumbs over her nipples and look into Savannah's eyes, searching for any sign of self-consciousness or fear and find none. She is breathing hard, her hands linked around my neck. She nods once, twice, and wraps her legs tighter around my waist.

"Jess," she whispers, and I think I might explode. "Jess, please."

"Please what?"

“I don’t know. Just touch me. Don’t stop touching me.”

I fill my hands with her breasts, squeezing and kneading, completely lost in her. She arches her back, pushing her breasts into my hands, and I slide a hand down to her hips. She presses her mouth to mine, her breath fevered and desperate.

“What are you doing to me?” she whispers, and her statement mirrors my thoughts. All I can do is shake my head. I can feel her body shaking, although at this point it could be either of us. I wrap my arms around her, trying to hold it together. Silently, I thank God we are in a public place; if we were alone right now, there’s no way I could have stopped.

“Why did you stop?” she says with her strange ability to read my thoughts.

“We’re in public,” I say, trying to keep a straight face. “This isn’t exactly the place I want to make love to you.”

“You want to make love to me?”

She doesn’t say it in a falsely modest tone of

voice, just in a way that makes me feel like she's asking a totally honest question. So I decide to give her a totally honest answer.

"Yes," I say quietly, watching her face for her reaction. Her cheeks are still flushed and her face is serious.

"Well, the feeling is mutual," she says, breaking the seriousness of the mood by disentangling her legs from my waist and jumping back into the water. She shakes her wet hair out and turns her face to the sky.

"There are so many more stars at home," she sighs.

"I'll bet. There has to be less smog in the middle of the redwood forest."

"There's none," she says simply. "It's perfectly clear, just stars and sky. In the summer, you can lie out and look for shooting stars."

I wonder how many wishes she's made those summer nights, searching for shooting stars. I wonder if any of them have ever come true.

Savannah reaches for my hand and I stand behind

her, holding her tight. We stand there for a few moments, and I try to absorb the tornado currently raging in my head and body. On the one hand, I want to take her home now and lose myself in her body; but on the other hand, I don't want to rush things. We barely know each other. I need more time to process everything.

She links her fingers with mine and leans her head back against my chest.

"Take me to your place," she says, and every rational thought in my mind evaporates.

CHAPTER 13
jesse

“I’ve only seen your house full of people,” says Savannah as we walk inside. It was only a ten-minute walk down the beach to my place. I opened the back door and let us in that way.

“It looks bigger,” she says, spinning in the living room. The sleek, modern look of my beach house suddenly looks cold in comparison to Savannah’s tiny house that she shares with two other people. I miss the wind chime that’s made with sea glass the exact shade of her eyes. She stops spinning and shivers.

“You’re cold,” I say. “Come with me.” I take her hand, the same way I did at the party, and she doesn't fight it. I lead her up the stairs, across the landing, and down the hallway to my bedroom. She steps inside.

"This is better than I remember it, too," she says. "It's huge." She catches sight of the balcony and heads straight for it, like a child. She slides open the huge double French doors and steps outside as I follow behind her. The backdrop of the balcony is a sky lit with stars meeting the dark expanse of the sea; it seems to go on forever.

"This is beautiful," she whispers. "Really, Jess. It's perfect."

"I've seen better views," I murmur, and she rolls her eyes but I see her cheeks redden. She shivers again, and I lead her inside, closing the door behind us. Having her in my bedroom again is driving me crazy. She walks over to my bed on her tiptoes, resting a hand on the dark wood baseboard. I walk toward her, pulling her hair over one shoulder so I can kiss her neck. I reach around and knead her hips at the same time, nudging her head to the side. She arches her back against me.

"Shower with me," she says, turning to face me, and I raise an eyebrow at her.

"If you try and tell me one more time that we need to take it slow or be cautious, I'm going to kill you," she says, reading me perfectly. "Don't second guess this." And for once in my life, I don't analyze or question or hesitate. I just do what she says and I let her lead me across the dark floors through the archway to the bathroom.

"Wow," says Savannah. "I should have guessed."

The bathroom is easily as large as my bedroom, all marble and black granite. The shower is glass with showerheads on two walls, plus a bench and shelf carved into the marble. The bathtub is separate, a huge Jacuzzi with steps leading to its raised position, with a huge window behind that looks out over the ocean. The sinks spout water out of dark, honey-colored amethysts and the enormous mirror illuminates both of us from head to toe.

"Too much?" I ask, but she shakes her head.

"It's insane, but it's beautiful. I love it."

"The floors are heated," I say, reaching for a box

on the wall. "We can turn them on so your feet won't be cold when you get out. Oh, and the sauna is around the corner from the bath. If you're into that."

Savannah sighs and spins in another circle, taking it all in. She stops and faces me, her drying hair in a wild halo that falls nearly to her waist.

"I feel like I'm in a dream," she says quietly, her words echoing off the walls.

"Me, too," I say. I cannot take my eyes off of her.

She looks me in the eye and reaches for the hem of her shirt, slowly tugging it up and over her head. For the first time, I see her in the light, sober, just the two of us standing here. I lose track of everything except how incredibly sexy she looks in nothing but her tight black pants. Her cheeks are flushed and heated. As I watch, she hooks her thumbs into the waistband of her pants. I am standing inches from her, afraid that if I touch her she'll fade away, because this doesn't feel real at all, but at the same time, it feels like the only real thing in the world.

"Are you sure?" I can't help but ask. She just tilts

her head and her lips curve up as she slides her pants down her legs. I have never seen anything as sensual as Savannah undressing for me without a hint of self-consciousness or fear. She stands in front of me and my eyes run over every part of her body, noticing things I've never seen before, like the birthmark that rides high on her thigh, and the way her waist curves into her hips. I reach toward her, running my hands down her back and then down lower. She shudders and shifts toward me and I smile.

"Do you want to me to touch you?"

"Yes," she whispers. "Please."

I kiss her neck, then her collarbone, then her breast, as I slowly lower myself to the ground until I am squatting in front of her. I look up at her and she's already breathing hard, tangling her hands in my hair. I wrap my arms around her waist, squeezing and fondling her perfect ass in my hands as I kiss the junction of her thighs.

"Jess," she says, her voice breathy and light, and I know she wants this as much as I do.

I kiss the top of each thigh, my tongue caressing

the tender skin, and her fingers weave through my hair. She can't stop moving, shifting her weight from foot to foot as her hips writhe beneath my hands.

"Stand still," I whisper, and she huffs out a breath.

"I can't," she says, and I smile.

I kiss my way from the top of her thigh to the junction between them again, and then flick my tongue so I can taste her for the first time. She cries out, her fingers pulling at my hair. I stand up, sliding my hands up her body again and she immediately wraps her arms around my neck and kisses me so hard I almost fall over. I can't stop running my hands over her, up her back and into her hair only to fall down again to her ass. Her tongue slides into my mouth and her teeth nip at my bottom lip. My body is straining against the confines of my clothing, and I step away from her and start working at the button of my jeans. She brushes my hands away and undoes it herself. I strip off my hoodie, tossing it onto the floor, and she reaches for the hem of my T-shirt and pulls it over my head. She stares at me, running her hands over my stomach. I flinch at her cold hands.

"Sorry," she says, grinning, and I shake my head. She grabs my waistband and pulls my pants down my legs, boxers and all. I am hard as fucking stone and her eyes fall as she stands up, her lips parting. She reaches for me, takes me in hand, and I groan as her hands grasp my body. She kisses my chest, moving her hands over me, and I grip her shoulders.

"Easy, Savannah," I say. Her touch is so intense it's almost too much for me to handle.

She ignores me, her hands moving over my skin, and I pull away from her. I sweep her up in my arms, her breasts crushed against my chest and my arms locked under her. She runs her hands through my hair and kisses me fiercely as I walk out of the bathroom and back into the bedroom.

"What happened to the shower?" asks Savannah into my hair.

"It can wait."

I drop her on my bed, and she stretches luxuriously

against the comforter, her naked body bright against the dark blue sheets.

"I could sleep on this forever," she says. "So comfy."

"Who says you'll be sleeping?" I murmur, leaning down to kiss her. I pull her down to the edge of the bed so her legs are hanging off the side and I'm standing above her. I yank her hands above her head using one hand, thrusting her breasts up, and use my mouth on her. She whimpers, grinding her hips against mine as I suck and tease one of her nipples. My free hand skims over her body, spreading her legs apart. She tangles her fingers through my hair again as she gasps. I caress the top of her thigh, nudging her legs apart. Slowly my hand slides against her inner thigh, where the skin is so soft. Savannah gasps, and my fingers finally touch her. Her whole body tenses, writhing against my fingers. I am fighting for control, but it's too much, and finally I stride to the nightstand and yank a drawer open. I rip open the package and roll the condom over myself as I walk back over to the bed. Savannah is sprawled on the bed, her cheeks flushed. One arm is thrown over her eyes and her legs are still spread. I run my hands down her thighs, and she looks up at me.

"What are you waiting for?" she asks, her voice husky. I smile and lower myself onto the bed with her under me, my elbows on either side of her head. I kiss her softly and reach down, stroking her, and she reaches for me in turn and guides me into her, inch by inch, until we are connected. I hold her face in my hands, my thumbs at her temples and my fingers tangled in her hair as I watch her face. She moans as I shift inside her, biting her bottom lip, and I kiss her hard. She wraps her legs around my waist and gasps as I start to move, and, fuck, it's incredible.

"Jess," she whispers, and as she kisses me I feel her nails dig into my back.

"Fuck," I whisper, and she moans. I start to really move, faster and faster, and her hips rise to meet mine. I lean back so I can see her face. Her eyes are closed, her lips parted, and her cheeks are rosy.

“Look at me,” I growl, and her eyes flick open. They are a blurred green and I know she is as lost in me as I am in her. I thrust into her and she arches her back, reaching up to press her lips to my throat and I lose all control, all sense of reality. There is nothing but her.

I open my eyes to the pink haze of early morning and the too-warm weight of Jesse Sharpe. He turns in his sleep, shifting away from me, and I frown. I was too hot, but it was nice to have him so close. I stretch out on my side of the bed, letting the silky sheets cool my naked skin. I guess we never managed to put pajamas on last night. Or take a shower, for that matter. I touch my lips with my fingertips; they are still a little swollen from his kisses. My body feels relaxed and worn out and I know without looking that my hair is a mess. Jesse turns over in his sleep again so he's facing me and I can't help but stare at him. I take advantage of his vulnerability—something he never displays to me—his sculpted face, that wicked mouth, not to mention his body.

My mind goes back to the night before, pulling his shirt off of him, and my mouth waters. He has the most perfect body and now I've seen all of it: tight abs, broad shoulders, muscular chest, and all that dark hair. I slide out of bed, trying not to wake him, and he shifts as I move but doesn't open his eyes. It's early still, probably about five a.m. They're filming today, but not any scenes where I'm needed, and not until later in the day. I walk over to the balcony doors, unlatch them and step outside into the pre-dawn light. The air is warm on my body as I look down at the beach. Waves kiss the shore and retreat, their white foam just visible in the pale light sneaking into the sky. I lean on the railing. I could get used to a view like this. I shake my head in almost the same instant; I know that a house like this, wealth like this, is never something I could get used to. When I stepped in here last night I was overwhelmed, by him and everything that comes along with him. It's what he's accustomed to, but not me. I shake my head again and retreat to the bathroom.

I flip on several of the huge nozzles and step inside the shower as the glass walls begin to steam up. There is enough room in here for most of the cast to shower together. I reach for some of his shampoo and sniff it; it smells like him. I hope he doesn't mind if I use some. I shrug and pour some into my hand and lather it into my hair. Of course, it's some European brand I've never heard of before. I wonder how much a bottle costs? I gasp as a hand suddenly snakes around my waist.

"You're up early," he murmurs into my ear, standing behind me. "Are you using my shampoo?"

"Yes," I gasp as his tongue invades my ear.

"Allow me," he says, and he begins to massage my scalp, rubbing the shampoo in. I groan; his hands are magic. He moves to my shoulders, massaging them gently, and then slides his hands around to flick his thumbs slowly over my nipples. My eyes fly open and I shift against him. I can feel him growing hard behind me and I'm instantly ready. I don't know what Jesse is doing to me, but I am already a slave to his touch. I reach behind me and find his erect body, stroking it with the soap still on my hands. He groans and slides his hands down my body, gently spreading my thighs.

"You're happy to see me," he says, and I feel him grin into my neck.

"Seems I could say the same," I gasp, and he chuckles. I hear bottles bump into each other and he squirts something else into his hands and begins to rub it into my hair.

"What is that?"

"Conditioner," he says. "Don't move." He runs his hands through my hair and then spreads a washcloth over my skin. Before I can ask, he says "body wash," and then continues. He scrubs my shoulders, down my back to my waist and around to my hips and then up again, making me gasp as the soft cloth flows over my breasts. They are overly sensitive, yearning for his touch. The cloth covers every inch of me, even going down my legs. I turn around, facing Jesse, and take the cloth from him.

"Your turn," I say. One side of his mouth curves up in that half-smile that always wreaks havoc on my insides, and he stands still as I smooth the wash-cloth over him in turn. I pass it over his strong shoulders, down his stomach, and over his erection as he grins at me.

"Want to wash my hair?" he asks, and I nod. He pours shampoo into my hand and I reach up on tiptoe to wash his hair. He closes his eyes and leans into my touch and then ducks under the water to rinse before letting me have my turn. My hair falls down my back in silky curls, free of the saltiness from last night. As I tilt my head under the spray, Jesse's hands don't stop touching me, running from my breasts to my hips and my butt, and then up again, so that when my hair is finally clean I am gasping for breath. I reach behind me blindly and turn the water off, and Jesse's mouth is already on mine. Our bodies are slick and wet, sliding against each other. I link my arms around his neck to press my body closer to his. My nipples are hard as cold air floods the shower, and they slide against his chest as he wraps his arms around my waist and lifts me so my toes are inches above the shower floor. He carries me out of the shower and lays me down on the heated floor, the bed too far for either of us to consider. A Sherpa rug cradles my head as he kisses my inner thighs, nudging my knees apart. I writhe beneath his touch, needing him, and he presses a kiss to one of my hips.

"Jess," I say, "Jess, please."

I moan as his tongue finally begins to move, licking and sucking as he holds my legs apart. I should have known his tongue would be just as magical as his fingers. I feel myself building higher and higher until the pleasure is almost too much to bear, but then all too quickly he stops. He did that last night, too, pulling away before I'd really had my fill. He slides over me, ending up with his elbows on either side of my face as he kisses my neck. I reach up to kiss his shoulders, running my hands over him. He leaves abruptly. I hear the nightstand drawer opening and the tear of a wrapper. He comes back in with the condom in his hand and I sit up.

"Let me," I say, and his eyes widen but he hands it to me and I rise to my knees in front of him. I take him in my hand, enjoying his sharp intake of breath, and then I can't resist leaning forward to swirl my tongue around him. He hisses out a breath between his teeth, and I grip his hips in my hands, holding him in place.

"Savannah," he says, and strokes my hair. I continue to slide my tongue over him as he cradles my head. I am elated just to be making him feel this way. Finally, he stops me and backs away to slide the condom on. When I look up at him again, his eyes are dark.

"Lay back," he says roughly, and I lay down on the tile, my head on the rug, and he kneels between my legs. My hands flex against the warm floor as his body presses against me and I close my eyes.

"Open," he hisses. "I want you to look at me."

I open my eyes again, but everything has gone blurry as he slides into me in one smooth motion.

"You okay?" he says, and I can see the concern in his gaze, but I nod.

"Yes," I say. "I'm fine. Please, Jess." My voice trails off as he starts to move and my hips answer his. His eyes are the darkest blue I've ever seen, locked into mine, and I am spellbound. There are no thoughts in my head; I am all feeling, all sensation, totally connected to him. My body begins to quiver around him, so sensitized from his mouth, and I whimper. It's so much: his hands in my hair, his skin against mine, the rush inside my body.

"Yes," he whispers, "yes," and we both fall together.

CHAPTER 15
savannah

We lie there on the bathroom floor for so long I lose track of time. I'm comfortable even with his weight on me, and the rug beneath my head is thick and soft. I'm drifting on a high that I can't even begin to describe. So much has happened since I've left home, since I met Jesse. I've learned so much about him, but I know so much more is beneath the surface. Our lives may be different, but who cares? I've never felt so alive, so excited, and so electric in my life. No way am I giving up this feeling. I run my hands along Jesse's back. I don't know where this is going, but I know I don't want it to stop. I do need to get home, though. I like being around him, but he makes my mind fuzzy. I want to go and be by myself for a while. Even as I start to shift underneath him, the front doorbell buzzes, the sound reverberating through the entire house. Jesse lifts his head from my chest.

"What the hell?" he mutters, standing up and grabbing a towel. "The housekeeper will see who it is." A moment later, there is a knock at Jesse's bedroom door. With a quizzical glance at me, he opens it wide enough to speak to her. I jump up and grab a robe that was hanging on the wall of the bathroom. It's obviously Jesse's—it hangs past my ankles. I hear Jesse speaking to someone, and then he shuts the door again.

"My dad is here," he says, frowning.

I have a minor heart attack.

"Here? Now?"

"I guess . . . He said he would be here tomorrow morning, to visit, but he isn't known for his reliability," says Jesse affectionately. "He probably forgot."

"Oh," I say. I don't know what my role is here. "Should I go?"

"Yeah, I was just going to sneak you out the back door." Jesse rolls his eyes. "Come and meet him."

I fold my arms, aware that in the bathrobe I look as intimidating as a mouse.

"Maybe I don't want to."

"You don't want to meet my dad?"

"No, sure, I'll meet him," I sigh, waving my arm in the air. "I just don't like it when you get all bossy."

"Am I bossy?" Jesse is grinning now, scrutinizing me with amused eyes.

"Yes," I answer. "And it's fine in bed, but not otherwise."

"No," he murmurs. "You are not one to be ordered around."

"I'm glad you understand that about me."

I crinkle my nose at him and set about getting dressed as best I can. If I'm going to meet his dad I may as well try to look decent.

"Are you nervous to meet him?"

Jesse hands me a sweatshirt that I yank over my head. It will do.

"No," I answer, trying to smooth my hair in the mirror. In the reflection, he looks surprised. "Why would I be? Is he mean?"

"No, not at all."

"Then, no. I'd like to meet him. Maybe I can ply him for information about you."

I'm wearing my yoga pants from last night, and Jesse's sweatshirt. My hair is wild, like always, but I've pulled it back as best I can. Without a hair dryer and some makeup, it's not going to get much better than this.

I nod, and Jesse presses a brief kiss to my forehead before leading me downstairs. His father is sitting on one of the couches in the living area, sipping a cup of coffee. He stands up as Jesse and I come in.

"Jesse!" He wraps Jesse in a bear hug, slapping his back, and I smile. He is wearing a button-up shirt with a bow tie and silver-rimmed glasses. He is thinner and lankier than Jesse, but with the same dark hair. "How are you? Sorry I'm here so early.

Damned secretary messed up the dates and I completely forgot . . . And who's this?"

Without waiting for Jesse to make what could potentially be an awkward introduction, I step forward.

"I'm Savannah," I say, smiling. This man is impossible to be nervous around. "I'm a friend of Jesse's." His father steps forward and hugs me like he just hugged Jesse, and then steps back with a huge smile.

"It's a pleasure, Savannah," he says. "I'm Blaine Sharpe, Jesse's dad. I'm sorry to have surprised you this way."

"It's no problem," I say. "I was on my way out."

"Can you stay for a cup of coffee before you go?"

I glance at Jesse, who shrugs, but he is giving me one of his half-smiles, so I shrug back.

"Sure," I say. "Coffee sounds great."

Before I know it, I am in an animated conversation with Jesse's dad about my hometown. As it turns out, he is from southern Oregon and knows the area. He is so kind and so interested in me, and it's obvious he adores Jesse. I love him on sight. Finally, I stand and set my empty cup down.

"It's been wonderful meeting you, Mr. Sharpe, but I really should go," I say, and he stands with me.

"Thank you for staying," he says warmly. "I hope to see you again before I leave."

"I would love that," I say, and I mean it.

"I'll walk you out," says Jesse, and we head to the foyer.

"Well, you certainly charmed him," says Jesse wryly, looking at me with raised brows.

"Are you surprised?"

"I guess not," he chuckles. "You charmed me, too."

I roll my eyes, but my heart warms. He's charmed me, too, even if I won't admit it to him yet.

"Can I offer you a ride home?" he asks. "I'd walk you or take you myself, but with my father here . . . "

"I'll walk," I say. "I'll go the way we came last night. It's early, the beach won't be crowded yet."

"Are you coming Friday?" he asks me, and I'm caught off guard.

"Coming to what?"

"Everyone is going to a new club that just opened in LA. We told you about this during filming yesterday."

I think back . . . That must've been when I was stuffing croissants in my mouth and watching Jesse in his board shorts.

"Oh," I say. "Everyone is going? Sure, I'll go, but Jesse—I'm not twenty-one."

"I know," he says. "It doesn't matter. You'll be coming as a part of the cast."

"Do I qualify for that? I'm just an extra."

"Yes," he says. "You and Paige and Sophie are all invited. You can use my driver again, if you'd like."

"You're not going to come with me?" I feel a vague stab of disappointment.

"No," he says. "I don't want people to know."

"Why?"

"I just don't," he says, running his hands through his hair. "I want to keep it private for a while."

I frown. I don't necessarily want people knowing my private business either, but I don't care *that* much. Then again, we haven't defined what is going on between us. It would be complicated to try and explain it to everyone. I shrug.

"Alright," I say. "Whatever works."

Jesse leans down to kiss me, and it starts lightly but escalates so quickly that when we pull away I'm breathing hard and his hands are already in my shirt.

"Jesus," he breathes, and I know what he means—this is so intense. How am I going to hide this at the party?

"I'll see you later, then," he says.

I look up into his blue eyes. "Yes," I say. "And I'll be at the party."

"Will you be wearing that gold dress again?"

I raise an eyebrow. "Did you like that one?"

"Very much."

"We'll see. I like to keep you guessing."

He studies me, one side of his mouth quirking up in my favorite smile.

“’Bye, Jesse.” I kiss him once, twice, with a hand on his jaw, and then walk down the steps toward the beach.

"No, no, no. Not that one. Try the red one instead."

I am standing in Paige and Sophie's room Friday afternoon, trying on dresses for tonight's party from Paige's endless supply. She has so many clothes that not even half of them can fit in the tiny closet she shares with Sophie. I pull on the ruched red dress and spin for both of my roommates. Paige shakes her head again.

"No, no," she mumbles. "Not quite . . . "

"I can't believe your life, 'Vannah," says Sophie for the hundredth time.

"Try this." Paige shoves a silky blue-green dress

into my arms. I stand and pull it on, spinning again, and Sophie claps.

"It's perfect," she squeals. "Paige, tell her it's perfect."

"It is," Paige agrees. "It brings out your eyes."

"So, no one but us knows what's going on?" Sophie asks.

"Nope."

"Is that weird?"

"A little," I admit. "But we don't really know what's going on between us, anyway."

Paige frowns.

"I guess we'll see how it plays out tonight," she says slowly. "You're a terrible liar, Savannah. What if you get a few drinks in you and end up all over him?"

"I can control myself," I say defensively. "It'll be fine."

"What would your life be like if you married a celebrity?" Sophie muses. "You would have people following you constantly—I mean the media and stuff."

"I'm not going to marry him," I laugh. "I want to see the world."

"He's seen most of it," says Paige. "He could take you."

"I'm still worried she's going to blow their cover tonight," says Sophie.

As they start to talk about the party, I finger the hem of the silky dress. The more I think about hiding my feelings in front of everyone tonight, the more nervous I get. Jesse and I have had a whirlwind week. Between filming and spending time together I feel like I'm leading a double life. And hiding our relationship hasn't been easy. I've noticed other people on set starting to give me strange looks when my gaze lingers on Jesse for too long, or when he smiles at me. It feels uncomfortable and strange to have to play this game, but at the same time I understand the need for secrecy. A part of me, though, wishes that Jesse would say, "Screw the paparazzi!" and walk in with me on his arm.

I sigh—wishful thinking. I see the way he looks at me, though, especially after we make love, and I know he's feeling what I'm feeling. It doesn't matter who knows and who doesn't as long as I remember that. I strip Paige's dress off and head into my room to put on a bikini. I want to catch a few waves. Some time alone in the water sounds like heaven right now.

I'm sitting on my board in the open water, surrounded by sea and sky. I let the waves flow under me, lifting and releasing me over and over again. I run my hands through my wet hair. What Paige said keeps running through my mind: *He's seen most of it. He could take you.* I just met Jesse, and I have an agenda for my own life that I'm not sure will be compatible with his, should things get more serious. I don't want paparazzi following me constantly, running bullshit stories about me in the media. I just want to be *me.* I don't really care if word gets out about Jesse and I, but I don't want to be splashed all over *Entertainment Weekly* as Jesse's new girl of the month. I shake water out of my ears and breathe in deeply. I need to relax. No matter what, I will live my life exactly how I want to—that is what I need to worry about. I like Jesse a lot and he likes me too, and right now that's all that matters. With the thought sill nagging in my mind, I paddle quickly and catch a nice set wave and ride it all the way back to the shore.

"How long is this going to take?" I whine, twisting around in my chair.

Paige has a hold of my hair and a curling iron and has been holding me hostage for the past hour.

"You have so much hair," says Paige. "That's why this is taking forever. Just hold still, I'm almost done."

I sigh, flipping around. This small space is so different from Jesse's luxurious bathroom. I scowl. Sophie got hold of my face, too, and now I'm wearing dark eyeliner and eye shadow to match. She did a wonderful job, as always, but I cannot sit still for this long.

Finally, Paige sets down the curling iron.

"Ta-da!" Paige turns me around in my chair.

"Holy shit," I breathe. My hair is a cascade of perfect waves, framing my face in a shining, golden glow. I twist, and the perfection continues down my back. "Paige, you're a miracle worker."

"Go put your dress on," she says. She and Sophie have been ready for an hour and Sophie has been in the kitchen mixing cocktails for the past ten minutes. I run to Paige and Sophie's room and slide the green dress on along with a pair of Paige's heels. They both walk in and Sophie hands me a drink.

"You look perfect," says Paige. "Let him try to pretend like he's not yours tonight."

"He's not mine," I say, but a part of me bristles at the thought of someone else having him. Sophie sips her cocktail; I think she's determined to get just as drunk at this party as she did at the last one. I take a cautious sip of my drink—Soph is notorious for making ridiculously strong cocktails and this one appears to be no different. Coughing, I make my way into my room and grab my phone where it's been lying on my nightstand all day. I unlock it and realize there is a text from Jesse.

I can't wait to see you tonight.

That's all it says, but I am on cloud nine. I can't wait to see him either.

"Savannah! The car is here!"

I down my drink in a single gulp, gasping as the alcohol burns its way down my throat, and head toward the door.

The club, Luxe, is one of the newest and most popular in Los Angeles. Our car pulls up to the curb and Paige, Sophie, and I hop out. The line is around the corner and the entire area is crawling with people.

"It's going to take forever to get in," says Paige, but as soon as the words leave her mouth, I see Jesse step out of his car. He stands on the curb in a black suit that makes my heart pound, looking absolutely perfect. The director gets out of the car next to him and the two begin to talk. The director gestures to us and Jesse turns and our gazes meet. He slowly smiles my favorite half-smile and my stomach does a somersault. The director waves us over, and Paige and Sophie and I head to where he and Jesse stand on the curb.

"Ladies," the director says, and we greet him, but I only have eyes for Jesse. He subtly reaches over and loops his arm around my waist. His touch instantly makes me shaky. I catch the first whiff of his scent and want to be in his arms so badly it is almost painful. It doesn't help that I've had a very strong drink already. Another car full of cast members pulls up and all of us are immediately ushered to the front of the line and into the club. It's almost completely dark inside, lit only by random spotlights above shadowed tables and the flashing lights over the dance floor. I walk in before Jesse and I feel him follow me closely, spreading a hand over my lower back. There were cameras and media outside, but in here it's so dark I don't think anyone will notice what's going on. Someone shouts something above the music about getting a table and some drinks and we head to a private area that's roped off by security. Not a single person has been asked for ID, and I am grateful. There are definitely perks to this lifestyle. I find Paige and Sophie again and together we order three vodka tonics. I don't drink liquor often and my head is already swimming. Jesse is engaged in conversation with several other main cast members, but I watch him out of the corner of my eye as the waiter promptly hands us our drinks. Jesse looks over at us and I think I see him frown. I take a large sip of my vodka tonic and shudder; it tastes like soap to me, but it's Paige's favorite drink.

"Let's go dance!" yells Sophie over the music, and Paige and I nod. We head down the stairs of our private area to the dance floor and a few other extras and cast members join us. Paige, Sophie, and I are in our own circle dancing and I'm having a great time until I feel hands on my hips. Thinking its Jesse, I grind against him and grab his hands, but as soon as I do I know I'm mistaken. I spin around and find some drunken guy trying to dance with me. He can barely stand up.

"No, thanks," I say loudly. "Maybe some other time!" He nods drunkenly and stumbles away, and

I see Jesse staring at me and he doesn't look happy. I turn back to Paige and Sophie and keep dancing.

"Who was that guy?" asks Paige.

"Just some drunk," I say, laughing. One of the other supporting actors approaches the three of us. I think it was the one Sophie was making out with at Jesse's party.

"Would you ladies like another round?"

"Yes!"

An hour later, I am four drinks in and much drunker than I was at Jesse's party. I cut myself off, waving another waiter away with a tray of drinks and head back to the dance floor to find Paige and Sophie. As I'm walking, I feel the same meaty hands around my waist. I turn around, more unsteadily than last time, to find the same drunk guy trying to follow me onto the dance floor.

"I said, no thanks!" I say to him loudly. He just ignores me and tries to pull me onto the dance floor. I try to dislodge his hands from my waist, but he's a big guy and I'm not having much of an effect.

"I believe she said she didn't want to dance," says a cold voice, and I look up into Jesse's face.

"She's dancing with me," says the big drunk guy, and I roll my eyes.

"No, she isn't," says Jesse calmly, but I see him set his jaw. The big drunk guy looks at me, and then at Jesse, and stumbles away. Jesse stares at me, his lips curving upward.

"Come with me," he says, and he takes my hand and leads me out a side door into the cool air of the night. We are in an alley on the side of the club, so no one is around that I can see. I gulp cold air like water, trying to clear my head.

"Are you alright?" Jesse asks, and I nod, but everything is getting fuzzier by the minute.

"Why did you bring me out here?" I ask. "Someone will notice we're gone."

"Do you know that guy?"

I stare at him. Is he serious?

"No, I don't know him."

"I didn't like the way he was acting with you."

I toss my hands into the air.

"I don't know what you want me to say. I didn't ask him to try and dance with me."

"I wanted to kill him when he put his hands on you."

Even in my inebriated state, I can see his eyes darken.

"Nothing happened," I say. I reach up to touch his face, and he leans his cheek into my hand. I'm so surprised by the way he's acting. I've never seen this possessive side of him.

"We don't even know what we are exactly," I say. "I don't know how I'm supposed to act or if you're even allowed to be mad at me."

His mouth quirks up again and he shoves his hands in his front pocket and studies me. He looks so perfectly sexy that I lose my train of thought.

"I know what you mean," he says. "This is new territory. I didn't think I was ready to define it."

"I'm not trying to force you into anything."

"I know," he says, running a hand through his hair. "Look, Savannah. It's not that I don't want to be exclusive with you, it's just important to me that, for now, our relationship stays quiet."

"Why?"

"Because I love having something to myself for once in my life," he snaps, and my eyes widen. "What is between you and me is different, it's special, and I want it to stay that way. I don't want the whole fucking world knowing about us, dissecting our relationship, spreading bullshit rumors. I want you to myself."

All I can do is stare at him, but as I look into his eyes I sway and stumble slightly in my heels. Jesse grabs my arm.

"How much have you had to drink?"

"I'm fine," I say, but he raises his eyebrows at me and I give in.

"About four," I admit. "I don't feel very good."

"Where are your friends?"

"Dancing."

"If you want to come home with me, you should tell them you'll be leaving."

I want to tell him off for being bossy, but his eyes

are mesmerizing and his bed is starting to sound a million times better than staying in the club. I head back inside and let Paige and Sophie know I'm leaving with Jesse. They hug me and say they're having our driver take them back to the house in a little bit. I go out the side door and there is Jesse, waiting for me. He takes off his suit jacket and drapes it around my shoulders and then leans in, cups my face in his hands, and kisses me so hard I lose all awareness of anything else. His mouth is possessive, controlling mine with hands and tongue, and my knees start to shake. I wrap my arms around his waist and enjoy feeling possessed by Jesse: it's new and I'm not sure why it's happening, but it makes me feel so wanted. The only thing that worries me is that I want him to be protective because he cares about me, not because he's controlling. I want him to care about me just for being me.

A car pulls up on the street ahead of us, and Jesse looks around but there is still no one to be seen other than a few people walking to their cars. Jesse takes my hand and leads me to the car, opening the door for me, and I slide inside. It's warm inside and it feels so good for my aching feet to be sitting down. Jesse slides in and closes the door, and the car begins to move. I close my eyes, fighting the dizziness that's engulfing my body, and reach down to pull my shoes off before leaning my head on Jesse's shoulder.

All too soon we arrive at his place and he helps me out of the car and into his bedroom. As soon as he tugs his shirt off, I start to run my hands over his perfect body.

"Savannah," he says. "You're drunk. It's okay—I didn't bring you here for this."

"It's what I want." I look up into his eyes and tilt my mouth toward his. "Please."

He groans and takes my face in his hands and unzips my dress as my hands work at his belt. Every place he touches brings shivers of pleasure and before I know it we are on the bed and he is kissing me so hard I can't catch my breath. He grabs a condom and quickly rolls it on and then rises above me, kissing his way from my neck to my stomach with so much tenderness it makes my heart ache.

"Jess," I whisper, and he slides into me, perfectly slowly, and I groan as he fills me and starts to move. I wrap my legs around his waist and lean up to kiss the edge of his jaw, running my nails down his back as he buries his face in my hair.

"Savannah," he murmurs, and I tilt my hips up to meet his. We are so good together, and it makes me so happy to hear how much he wants me in just that one word. I lose myself in what we bring to each other. I am floating as he stops moving, and I am dimly aware of him pulling something soft over my body and turning the lights off. As he pulls me to him and holds me, I drift away, unsure if what's happening to me is a dream or reality.

She sleeps late after last night's drinking. I sit in sweatpants and a T-shirt on the bed next to her, my laptop on my lap so I can at least work a little before she wakes up. There's a charity event happening in another few weeks or so and I need to work out some details. I make a mental note to remind Jeremy about it. I find myself staring at Savannah more than my computer screen. Her hair is spread around her face while she breathes in and out. I pulled one of my T-shirts over her before she fell asleep last night and that's all she's wearing. Even compared to last night's outfit, she looks perfect. I shake my head. Last night was both heaven and hell.

When I saw her standing on the street in that dress I wanted to take her straight home and peel it off of her, then seeing her with that drunk asshole was even worse. I've never felt that way in my life, but as soon as he put his hands on her I saw red. My father was incredulous when she left yesterday.

"She's incredible, Jesse," he said, looking at me over the rims of his glasses. "Is she an actress?"

"No," I said. "She's not. We found her surfing on the beach and asked her to be an extra. She's just in LA for the summer."

"What about after that?"

I frowned, realizing I had no idea what her plans were after the summer.

"I don't know, actually."

"I've never seen you with someone like her. It's very refreshing, Jesse."

"Don't go seeing weddings and babies yet, Dad," I said wryly, and he chuckled. His words have been running through my mind ever since. My dad knows me better than anyone and I value his opinion. He's seen me date actresses, models, athletes, and out of them all, I know he prefers Savannah by far. Savannah rolls over in her sleep and nuzzles my leg with her nose before settling down into the mattress. I stroke her hair, amused. Her eyes flutter open and she gives me a sleepy smile. All I can think is, *Fuck*. I care about this girl. I didn't expect that.

"How are you feeling?" I ask her.

"Okay," she says, yawning. "A little headache but nothing unmanageable."

She pops out of bed and stretches before heading to the bathroom. I shake my head. Savannah is happier in the morning than anyone else I know. It's unnatural. She comes back into the room and flops down on the bed beside me, laying her head on my shoulder. We sit in silence for a few peaceful minutes, me still working on my computer with one arm, and with her in the curve of the other as the sun begins to shine in through the balcony doors. She twines her fingers through my hair and I close my eyes briefly at her touch.

"I'm going home in a few days," she says. "Just for a visit."

I frown. "Oh."

"Do you want to come with me?"

I look down at her. Her eyes are wide and hopeful, her bare legs curved on the sheets.

"Would I meet your parents?"

"Yeah, of course."

"Where are you from again?"

"Humboldt County."

"No, I know that. I mean the name of the city."

"Oh. Fortuna."

"Right." Never heard of it.

I think of the movie: there is a break in filming coming up due to some negotiation or other, but there is still plenty I need to do. Press conferences, interviews, guest appearances, photo shoots—I have it all planned for the next few weeks. There is a little flexibility in the near future, though, if I decided to rearrange my schedule. I'd like to see Savannah's hometown.

But I look into her sea-glass eyes, and it's not just that I want to see where she comes from and the place she calls home, it's that I'm finding it increasingly difficult to say no to her.

"Yes," I say, and her smile lights up her face. "I'd love to."

CHAPTER 19
jesse

A few days later we are headed north on the 5 in my Mustang with the top rolled down. She insisted on driving, so I'm sitting in the passenger's seat of my own car and still feeling disgruntled about it. When I see the speedometer hit ninety, I start to quietly panic.

"Savannah, slow down. Jesus."

If I were driving ninety miles an hour I wouldn't be concerned, but with her at the wheel the circumstances are different.

"Oh, you're no fun," she mutters, but she is grinning from ear to ear. Her hair is tied back with a headband and is still flying in a wild cloud around her face in the wind. I hold my phone up in the air. It still shows no bars. I haven't been in a place without cell service in longer than I can remember and I'm on edge about the fact that neither Jeremy nor anyone else from the set can reach me.

"Relax," says Savannah, reaching for my hand. "You'll have service when we're closer to my house."

It's unnerving sometimes, how easily she reads me.

"How far are we?"

"About two hours away."

We left at five this morning and now it's nearly three in the afternoon. I've never been this far north in California before and I'm trying to take it all in. While Los Angeles is all buildings and freeways, cars and people, the closer we get to Savannah's hometown, the more remote the landscape becomes. It's beautiful, with mountains covered in massive redwood trees, winding rivers, and above it all, a dark blue sky. When I asked Savannah if there would be traffic, she almost cracked a rib laughing.

"No way," she said when her laughter finally stopped. "We'll be the only people on the road."

We wind through an area she calls Richardson Grove, which curves between the biggest trees I've ever seen in my entire life. They tower hundreds of feet above us, some so wide that they're more like a building than a tree.

"Wait until you see the ocean here," says Savannah. "You're going to love it."

Her cheeks are rosy and she hasn't stopped smiling since we got inside the county line and it makes me happy to see her so excited. She's like a child, talking and gesturing with her hands the entire time, but it doesn't annoy me. She's never done anything to annoy me since I've known her and that's unusual for me. The more I know about her, the more I care about her, and that fucking terrifies me. Letting her take me to her hometown opens up another layer of her and, while I expected her to be nervous about that, she just jumped in headfirst the same way she does with everything. I love that about her—the way she follows impulse and doesn't hesitate to show who she really is. In fact, I don't think she could be anyone but herself if she tried.

"Almost there," she says, and I squeeze her hand.

Her parents are kind and welcoming and Savannah's house is red brick set way back in the redwood forest. I can see Savannah gets her hair from her mother and her eyes from her father, the opposite of myself.

"You have a beautiful home, Mrs. Taylor," I say, and she blushes, just as Savannah would.

"Please, call me Brenda," she says. She wears an apron that is smeared with some sort of frosting that Savannah immediately goes looking for in the kitchen. As my phone finally starts to receive the messages and emails I've missed on the drive, I excuse myself to the back deck to respond to everyone. I have to explain to Jeremy to tell my publicist to relax; there is little chance of me being followed by paparazzi in a place like this. When I've talked to Jeremy and arranged my new schedule for when we return to Los Angeles, I start to head back into the house, but pause when I hear Savannah speak my name.

"Mom, it doesn't matter that he's a movie star. He's still a person."

"Have you considered a future with him? Is that the life you want?"

"We're barely dating. Everything is very new."

"'Vannah, I see the way you look at him. It may be new, but he means a lot to you."

I am motionless, taking in every word. Savannah is quiet.

"He does," she finally says, so quietly I think I misheard her. "That's honestly all I know right now, Mom."

I can't stand eavesdropping any longer so I head into the living room as though I've just finished my phone conversation. Brenda's concerns mirror my own. In terms of a future between Savannah and me, there would be a lot to negotiate. We come from totally different worlds. But more and more, I want her to be a part of mine.

The next couple of days fly by as Savannah shows me her surfing haunts and favorite places in her hometown. We spend time with her parents and I see more and more of Savannah's past. She takes me surfing in Trinidad—both of us wearing wetsuits, I had to borrow her dad's—and shows me some of the most beautiful beaches I've ever seen. They are nothing like Southern California—completely remote, cold—and with towering sea cliffs and crashing surf unlike anything I've ever seen. I get used to it being just she and I, not having phone service very often. I feel completely out of my element here in this strange place where I'm disconnected from everything, but

Savannah steadies me. I never feel like I don't belong when I'm with her.

On our third afternoon I'm sitting with my feet buried in sand someplace Savannah calls Agate Beach when I realize how much I'm enjoying myself. Savannah is sitting next to me, her hair in a messy braid down her back. I can tell she is concentrating even through her dark sunglasses. Searching for agates is hard. They're these strange clear rocks that have been washed by the sea for so long they become almost completely translucent and most of them are tiny. We've been here for a half an hour and still haven't found one. Savannah sighs and crawls into my lap, winding her legs around my waist.

"I'm never going to find an agate this way," I say, already nuzzling her neck. The salty sea breeze lingers on her skin in a way that I love.

"You'll probably never find one anyway," says Savannah cheerfully. "Tourists are terrible at it. You haven't had to hone your vision your entire life the way I did."

"You haven't found one yet either," I point out, and Savannah pouts.

"You're distracting me," she says, kissing my jaw. It's a sunny day, but windy, and there are only a few other people on the beach, so far from us they're just spots on the horizon.

"You climbed onto my lap," I say, sliding a hand up the back of her shirt. "Don't act like you don't like it."

She grins, tilting her head back as I kiss her neck. It takes about two seconds of being close to Savannah before I lose track of everything else. Being away from reality like this is just making it worse. I'm starting to believe that we can stay like this forever.

Savannah sighs, linking her hands around my neck, and kisses me softly. She jumps up and heads down the beach to the edge of the waves and I follow.

"Let's move this way," she calls to me.

I'm following her, still scanning the sand when something catches my eye. I kneel down and gingerly grab the tiny rock from the sand. I'm not even sure it's an agate, but it looks like one to my inexperienced eye. It's a pale, pale golden color so clear I can see through it, with patches of white clouding certain spots. It's also tiny—I have no idea how I spotted it in the sand.

"Savannah," I call, and she turns around. "I think I found one."

She heads back over and takes the agate from my hand, turning it over in her fingers. She peers at it, holding it up to the light and I fight a smile. She looks like a female Indiana Jones in her ball cap, staring at a new batch of unseen treasure.

"This looks like one to me," she says finally. "I have to admit I'm impressed. I never thought a city boy like you would find one before me."

She slips the agate into my pocket, grinning at me.

"Well, well, well," I say. "Looks like you're a little out of practice."

Savannah just rolls her eyes, her mouth pouting,

but as she turns away I snatch her up and spin her in a circle.

"I want you to have it," I say, and Savannah immediately shakes her head.

"No way," she says. "You found it, and it's your first agate ever. I have a whole drawer at home."

She pulls the agate from my pocket and surveys it again before placing it in my hand. I swear the heat from her touch lingers there hours later, even after the sun is gone.

We head back to Savannah's house and have dinner with her parents. Her mom makes these things called apple fritters, basically deep-fried and battered apple rings dipped in sugar, and they're amazing. I'm sitting at the kitchen table staring at my phone and waiting to see if any calls come in during the brief time I have service when Savannah snags my hand.

"Do you want to go watch the sunset?" she asks.

"Only if you let me drive," I say, and she sticks her tongue out at me. I don't care. I nearly went into cardiac arrest on the way here and I'm not about to repeat the experience.

She guides me through a tiny town filled with grassy fields, cows, and old trucks, and then we are on a winding route to the sea. We pull up to where the road meets the beach and she jumps out of the car. The air is cold and biting, but the clouds are parting over the dark water and the sun is shining through as it sets. Savannah takes my hand and leads me all the way to the water. It hits my feet and I hiss at the chill of the waves, so intense my toes are already going numb.

"Don't go too far down the beach," says Savannah. "See how steep those cliffs are? That means the waves beat the sand hard and there's a strong undertow."

I have no desire to go any deeper than my ankles in this water anyway and I tell her so. She laughs, but she is shivering in the bite of the wind, and I wrap my arms around her as we watch the sky begin to darken and the pink of the sunset spread across the horizon.

My conversation with my dad flashes through my mind.

"What are your plans for when summer ends?" I ask quietly. Savannah stiffens slightly and glances back at me.

"I don't know," she says quietly. "Originally my plan was to travel when I had the money. With what I'm making as an extra, I'll be able to go sooner."

"Where do you want to go?"

"Everywhere," she says, a small smile pulling at her lips. "Italy, Thailand, Egypt, Ecuador. I want to see everything."

"I've been to a lot of those places," I say. "They were all incredible."

"Would you go with me?"

I pause, considering her question. My life is centered on my career and has been for years. The traveling I've done has been almost entirely due to movie sets or press events being in those areas. I could take some time off, but I'm not sure I'm ready to make that sacrifice. I'm excited about this movie and proud of the work I'm doing.

"I don't know," I say honestly. "I guess it depends."

She nods, but I see her face fall. "I understand."

"I can't just drop everything and disappear the way you can."

"Yes, you can," she says. "You absolutely can. Your life is your decision, Jesse. It's all about the way you want it to unfold."

"It's not always that simple, Savannah."

"Yes, it is. When you get down to what matters, your life is your choice. You have the power to make it anything you want."

I stay quiet, but her words resonate in my mind. She has such a different outlook on life than mine, and, even as I argue with her, I'm digesting her perspective. I know that life is what you make it, but I have obligations that I can't just abandon. Savannah stands quietly in front of me, sighing deeply as I hold her, and I can't stand to see her sad.

"I would love to see all those places with you," I say into her ear, and she turns toward me with a bright smile, her eyes searching my face. "Really, I would Savannah, it's just—"

"Look up," she whispers, interrupting me, and I look up at the sky. It is a canvas of orange, purples, and pinks, all blending together in a perfect combination. The light plays over Savannah's face and she turns in my arms so she is facing me. Everything else evaporates from my mind. I tilt her chin up and kiss her softly, and as her lips yield beneath mine I forget all the reasons I should walk away. All I can think is I never want to lose this. I twist my hands in her hair and yank her head back. She gasps and I kiss behind her ear and then down her neck. Her hands are already slipping up my shirt. She nips my lower lip and I groan. I fight for control, leaning my forehead against hers. She is breathing hard, her breath swirling into wisps of white in the dark as the sun fades behind us.

"I don't want to lose you," I whisper.

"I'm right here," she says, winding her fingers through my hair. She kisses me hard, our tongues intertwining, and she's yanking at my shirt.

"Savannah," I say, and she takes my hand and drags me through the sand to the car. I grin as we crawl into the backseat, feeling like we're about sixteen.

"I know," she says in the strange way she reads my mind. "Does it bother you?"

"Does it bother me that you want to have sex in the car? Please," I say. "I'm still a guy, Savannah. And you're still the most fucking beautiful thing I've ever seen."

She kisses me and our bodies twist together, the cramped space making the heat between us even more intense. The windows steam and Savannah's skin becomes slick under my hands. I yank her shirt over her head at the same time as she pulls my jeans off and she crawls on top of me, pushing me so I am sitting up against the seat. I grope for my jeans and pull a condom out of my back pocket and Savannah takes it and rolls it on, achingly slowly. She takes my face in her hands, kissing me fiercely, and I know she is putting everything she has into this—she is pouring her heart into my hands and asking me to take it. All I can do is run my hands over her body, giving what I can in return. She pauses, reaches for me, and guides me inside her, and the heat of it swamps me. I grip her hips in my hands as she moves over me, her forehead tilted against mine.

"Jess," she whimpers in that voice I love. "Jess . . . "

"I know," I say, because more and more I feel that I know what she means without her having to explain. I lose track of everything but Savannah's skin on mine as she takes control, locking her arms around my neck. Her eyes are blurry, locked on mine, and I wrap my arms around her as the rest of the world disappears.

I'm starting to get used to waking up every morning and heading out to some new adventure with Savannah. As the days pass, I'm even beginning to appreciate the way we can be completely immersed in each other without the world interrupting.

But, of course, reality is always just a phone call away. We are in the living room with Savannah's parents when my phone starts to buzz and Jeremy's name appears on the screen. I apologize, and as Savannah smiles at me, I step outside to take the call.

"Jeremy," I say, holding the phone to my ear. It's just starting to get dark outside.

"Jesse. We talked about that charity event a while back? It was originally scheduled for about a week from now."

"Yeah, I remember."

"Turns out the date we had was wrong. Someone put it down in the schedule incorrectly and it's been mixed up this whole time."

Jeremy sighs, and I don't bother asking who made the mistake. Knowing the way he runs the publicity team, they've been dealt with already.

"No one had the brains to figure it out until now, apparently," he continues. "Anyway, they're expecting you tomorrow night in Los Angeles."

"Are you serious? Tomorrow?" I rub my hand over my eyes. Savannah and I are supposed to stay at least a few more days.

"What exactly is the event again?" I ask. I try to ignore the pricks of annoyance spiking into my temples.

"It's a gala. It's a huge event, a charity ball. A black-tie affair. The press hasn't seen much of you while you've been filming and away on this little gallivant that you insisted upon. This is a perfect opportunity to leap back into the spotlight."

"If I go, I'm bringing Savannah."

Jeremy pauses. I can practically hear him tapping his fingers on his knee.

"That's not the worst idea, actually. She's new, different—an attention-grabber. People will want to know who she is, this new girl on Jesse Sharpe's arm. And she's stunning . . . she'll certainly look the part."

I feel a twinge of pride. Savannah is gorgeous, and she's mine. I want to show her off. Maybe it's time to introduce her to my world the way she's introduced me to hers.

"Count us both in," I say impulsively. "I'll wear a tuxedo, obviously, but she's going to need a dress."

"I can get somebody on it."

"Good. Let me know."

I hang up just as Savannah walks out to meet me on the deck.

"Hi, beautiful," I say, and she rubs her cheek against my arm like a cat.

"Hi," she murmurs. "Who was that?"

"Jeremy. There was a mix-up with one of my social obligations."

"Oh, really? What happened?"

"Well, I have something to ask you."

"Ask away."

"Would you like to go to a ball with me?"

She pauses, letting her hair fall down her back again and stares at me. I can almost see her heart shining out of her. She has the most expressive face I've ever seen.

"Did I just become Cinderella?" she asks.

I burst out laughing. "It's a charity ball," I explain. "A gala. Some of the cast members are attending and I'd like you to go with me."

"As what?"

"As what you are."

"Which is?"

I roll my eyes. She so obviously just wants to hear me say it.

"As my girlfriend, Savannah."

Her smile beams over me, like sunlight, and I can't help but smile in return.

"Yes," she says. "Yes, of course I'll go."

"It's tomorrow night."

She frowns and her face falls. "Tomorrow?"

"Yes. I know we were supposed to stay longer, but the event date was changed."

"Oh," is all she says.

"Is that okay with you?"

She shrugs, and it's hard for me to see her face in the fading light.

"You don't absolutely have to come," I suggest. "I could go by myself."

She is silent for a moment.

"I don't want that either," she says quietly. "Do we have to go? Is it that important?"

"Yes," I tell her. "And I committed to it."

Even in my ears I sound stilted and boring, and even worse, cold.

Savannah stares at me for a moment longer, and

I feel like an ass, but what I'm saying is true. I need to be there.

"I guess I'll tell my parents we're leaving tomorrow," she says, and then heads inside.

I stand on the deck for a few more seconds and then turn to head in after her just as my phone rings again.

"Yes," I snap, without bothering to look at who's calling.

"A fine way to greet your mother," says a smooth voice with more than a hint of bite.

"Oh," I say. "Hello, mother."

"I'll be in Los Angeles tomorrow night," my mother continues.

I can hear the click of swirled ice cubes in the background and it takes me right back to the rare times I saw my mother as a child.

"Oh?" I say politely. "For what purpose?"

"The same as you, darling. I'll be at the gala."

Jesus. My mother and Savannah—just what I need. They are polar opposites: you never know what my mother is really thinking, and Savannah's thoughts are written in block letters on her face. My mother is coldly beautiful, like new snow, while Savannah warms every room she walks into.

"Who are you bringing?" my mother asks, jolting me out of my thoughts. "Lila? Please not her again, dear. You're far too good for her."

"No."

"Oh good. Someone else? Anyone I know?"

I resist the urge to laugh. "No, mother—she doesn't exactly run in your circles. She's an extra in the movie, someone I met on the beach in LA."

Three seconds of silence stretch as my mother weighs my words, just as I knew she would.

"Lovely," she finally says, giving nothing away. "I'll see you both there."

It is both a promise and an order, and then there is the click of the line.

"Your mother will be there?" asks Savannah. I turn to see her standing in the doorway.

"Yes," I say. "Does that bother you?"

Savannah frowns, and I think she's annoyed. "Jesse, you always ask me questions like this. I'm a little nervous to go to the gala because I've never been to anything like it before, but no, I'm not scared to meet your mother. What you're really asking is if I'm scared to see what she thinks of me, and the answer is still no."

She sighs. "It's not that I don't want to make a good impression. It's just that I am who I am and she is who she is. I can't put on an act to try and be what she wants. All I can do is be myself. So there's really no point in worrying."

Her answer rocks me to the core.

I have spent my life surrounded by people whose careers depended on how well they played a character. I, myself, have learned to be a chameleon, changing myself to fit the necessary role or event at hand. I am floored by her logic, and it resonates within me in a way that is both uncomfortable and fascinating.

I've never met someone like Savannah, who is exactly who she is without having to think about it, without even having to try. It astounds and humbles me.

She reaches for my hand, brushing her lips over it, and I let her touch calm the storm inside me, as it always does.

The dress is blood-red, and as I'm zipped into it, the stylist paints my lips the same rich hue. It's floor-length satin, perfectly fitted, and so silky I'm afraid it could slide right off my heated skin. Antonio has come to do my hair, insisting that no one else knows it the way he does, and he's probably right. My hands fidget in my lap. I am happy to be going with Jesse tonight, but I'm still irritated about the way it happened. Our trip home was important to me and I felt as though he completely dismissed it as soon as another obligation presented itself. I tried to be understanding about it; I know this is his job, but it hurt my feelings. I felt as though I came second to his career and that feeling has stuck with me ever since, nagging at me. I try to push it from my mind; I want to enjoy this night. I'm here for Jesse and I want to make the best of it, whatever the circumstances.

Antonio adds one more curl, smoothing a tendril around my face. Makeup has already done their job—smoky gray has been swirled around my eyes, and my eyelashes are dark and lengthened. I haven't seen myself in two hours as they have me faced away from the mirror—Antonio's orders—so I can't fidget.

"Perfect," he says finally. Someone slips heels on my feet, a sparkling silver so delicate they might be made of glass.

"Can I please look at myself now?" I beg. "I feel like a china doll."

"Such impatience," sighs Antonio. "But yes. Turn around."

I stand on the silver shoes, balancing myself, and turn toward the mirror. My jaw drops. I don't know the person staring back at me. She is radiant: clinging satin against pale skin, bright eyes, carnation lips, and rosy cheeks. My hair falls in perfect curls nearly to my waist, artfully arranged over my shoulder by Antonio. This girl looks as though she's attended balls since she was old enough to walk, not someone who walked into the dressing room with feet still sandy from the beach.

"Holy fuck," is all I say, and Antonio fights a smile.

"You are absolutely stunning," he says, kissing my cheeks. "It's time to go." Someone else hands me a shawl for my shoulders and a silver clutch that matches my shoes. I hear footsteps and I spin toward the door. Jesse is walking down the hallway in a perfect black tuxedo, looking so confident and perfect that I can't take my eyes off of him. He looks up from a cufflink and stops in his tracks. His eyes travel over me from head to toe in such a possessive way that it makes the other people in the room seem like intruders.

"Savannah," he murmurs, his eyes piercing. "You look absolutely perfect."

My lips part as my heart flutters against my ribs.

I am sure my love for him is obvious because I feel it welling up inside me with such force. I'm not sure I can pinpoint the exact time that it happened, but I know it with so much clarity that it frightens me. I love this man.

He holds out his hand, smiling at me, and I take it without hesitation.

"That dress is perfect," he murmurs in my ear, and I shiver. "I can't wait to peel you out of it later."

"Good luck," I whisper back. "It's so tight you're going to have to tear it off me."

I head down the hallway as he stands motionless, stunned, I think, into immobility.

It's not until we arrive at the gala that the nerves hit. I am so excited and so on edge. I've never done anything like this before, but I will for him. He exits the car and holds out a hand for me. I can already see the flashing lights, hear the voices screaming at him, but he looks at me and I focus on the blue of his eyes and nothing else. I take his hand and as soon as I emerge from the car, the crowd erupts.

"Jesse, who's this new girl on your arm?"

"Jesse, is it true that Lila Swanson is now seeing Robert Law? Have the two of you broken it off?"

Jesse just holds my hand, seeming completely unfazed. Security flanks us as we make our way into the venue, and Jesse links his fingers with mine.

"It's a little overwhelming," he says apologetically, and I laugh.

"Just a little," I say. "But I'm alright."

"Champagne?" a waiter asks, and Jesse takes two flutes.

"To the most beautiful girl in the world," he says, giving me a slow smile. I smile back and his eyes lock on mine as we each take a sip.

"Jesse?" That voice sounds both familiar and foreign, as lovely as snowflakes, but with a chill. A woman walks toward us with flaming red hair and the most perfect face I've ever seen, dressed from head to toe in pale blue chiffon. I instantly know who she is: not only have I seen her in movies and on TV since I was a child, but she looks exactly like

Jesse. As she approaches us, I recognize his turquoise eyes in her sculpted face.

"Mother," says Jesse, and I can't help but think how formal a greeting that is. When I saw my mom last weekend I ran straight into her arms and instantly got covered in cookie dough.

"Jesse, darling. How wonderful to see you." She kisses him, and then turns to me. "And who's this lovely creature?"

She looks me over as though I'm a piece of fruit she's considering buying.

"This is Savannah Taylor," says Jesse, taking my hand. "Savannah, my mother, Eliza."

She takes my hand briefly and I feel the bite of her rings.

"Hello," I say, smiling at her. "It's great to meet you."

"And how did you two meet?"

"On the beach. I'm living in LA for the summer. Jesse thought I was drowning and tried to save my life. Really, he just got in the way."

Jesse raises his eyebrows at me and I crinkle my nose at him. I see Eliza's eyes widen slightly.

"How nice," she murmurs. "You seem to have quite an effect on my son. What will you do when the summer is over?"

Jesse frowns at her, and I'm surprised she'd ask such an awkward question.

"Well, I want to travel," I say slowly. "I know that much. But I haven't figured out the particulars yet."

"Jesse has another obligation practically right at the beginning of fall, don't you, dear?" says Eliza, and I am starting to hate her. "Another acting opportunity. We were just discussing it yesterday."

Jesse is openly glaring at her now and I feel like I am rooted to the floor. Is this a serious commitment he's making? Why hasn't he told me? But before anything more is said, the casting director walks up and immediately greets Jesse and me and her questions are stalled. The rest of the night flies by in a whirl of color and faces. I meet more celebrities than I could possibly absorb in one night and I feel more and more sick as the night goes by. I just want to get home and talk to Jesse, to get back to a place where it's just him and me and the rest of the world goes quiet. Eliza doesn't say anything more to me and I wonder what her issue is. She seems cold and calculating, completely unlike the warmth of Jesse's father. I resent her for making the evening stressful for me. I manage to distract myself with conversation and dancing in Jesse's arms, but by the time we are in the car and headed home, I am completely worn out. Jesse unbuckles my seatbelt and slides me onto his lap so my head is nestled on his shoulder.

"Tired, baby?" he asks, and my heart jumps at the endearment.

"Yes," I say. "Very."

"Did you have fun?"

His expression is concerned and watchful.

"Yes," I say. "But it was stressful, too."

"You mean my mother?" says Jesse. "Yeah. She has that effect on people."

I can see his jaw tighten as he talks about her and I sit up to face him.

"Was she telling the truth, Jesse?"

When he hesitates, I already know the answer.

"Yes," he says, "but nothing is finalized yet."

"What is it exactly?"

"Another movie, shot somewhere else in the States. It would start soon after the shooting ends for the one we're doing now."

Our conversation sounds strange in my ears: two strangers discussing completely separate plans for their future.

I'm not sure why I feel so betrayed, but a lump rises in my throat and lodges there, making it impossible for me to speak. When did Jesse's plans start mattering so much to me? I know the answer almost as soon as I ask it to myself. It changed when I started loving him.

"What's wrong?" he asks.

I just shake my head. "What about me?" I say quietly, turning to him, with eyes that are already becoming blurry with tears.

"What about you, Savannah?" asks Jesse. "Just

because I might sign on for this part doesn't mean we can't be together."

"I have dreams, too," I say. "I have plans of my own."

"I didn't know it would be such an issue to wait for a little while."

"You're not asking me to wait. If you asked that of me I would do it for you in a heartbeat."

"How am I not asking you to wait?" He runs his hands through his hair and the tension between us starts to build, a crescendo of voices.

"You aren't asking me. Your career is."

"What's the difference?"

"That's my point," I say. "There should be a difference."

He stares at me, his eyes starting to darken as he gets angrier.

"I would have considered waiting if it was you asking me, Jesse," I say. "*You.* But it's not you, it's your career. You ask but you won't give. You go to my house but cut the trip short. You'll fuck me but won't discuss the future. I would fit my life into yours."

Tears are blinding me now but I brush them away. I don't want him to see me cry. Jesse stares at me, his eyes full of some dark emotion I can't place.

"I didn't realize you were so upset about this gala," he says. "I didn't want to leave your parents' house early either, Savannah."

"But you did," I say. "You knew it would upset me and you did it anyway. And the only reason I came to this fucking gala was for you."

"It was an event for my career," he says.

"I know," I say. "I just wish you and your career could be separate sometimes. I just want to be with *you*. That night, on the beach, you said you didn't want to lose me. You said you wanted to see all the places I've dreamed about with me and now it seems like neither of those things are true."

"I do want to be with you," he says. "Savannah, you know that."

"I know you do," I say. "But on your terms, not mine. There has to be a middle ground, Jesse."

I stare at him, hoping against hope that he'll say what I need to hear, but he is like stone. What he said on the beach that night were promises to me, promises I held close, and now I can feel them fading to dust in my mind. I feel everything we've built up between us is beginning to fall away, like ashes in the wind.

"I don't know what you want me to say," he whispers.

My tears start to fall, against my best efforts. "I want you to give," I plead, fisting my hands in his shirt. "I want you to realize that everything that you think matters so much, matters much less than you and me."

His eyes are soft and full of pain, but I can see the doubt in them.

"Savannah, I have obligations. I have commitments and I have a life I've created. I want you to be a part of it."

"I can't," I whisper. "I can't only be a part of your world. You have to be a part of mine, too."

I look out the window and through bleary eyes I

can tell we are nearing Jesse's house, but I can't stay with him. I have to go, now, before I lose my nerve and he kisses me and convinces me to stay.

"Can you please drop me off?" I gasp to the driver, my voice raspy with tears. "Here is fine. I'll walk home."

"Savannah, you are not walking home from here."

"My house is right here," I plead. "Please, Jesse, just let me go."

His face is a mask of pain, but he pulls a shade over himself and I'm left with the shell of him. The person sitting next to me has completely withdrawn and I hate it more than anything. He could at least have the courtesy to show me his feelings. The driver pulls to the side of the road and I jump out, holding the perfect shoes in my hands.

"Savannah, your dress," says Jesse. "You can't walk home in that."

I explode.

"It doesn't matter!" I scream. I turn to face him as the wind yanks my hair out of its perfect arrangement. "Can't you see, it doesn't matter at all? Who cares about this stupid fucking dress?" He looks completely shocked, all color draining from his face, but I am livid. I know I am missing some of what he means, but I am past my breaking point. He has such a warped sense of the things that matter and the things that don't that I am afraid I will never be able to get him to understand. I turn my back on the car, on his perfect tuxedo, and his pleading eyes, and I walk into the wind.

It's been a week, and I am living without light. I click on my phone for the millionth time, but her name doesn't appear. I can't sleep. I toss and turn, and as soon as I drift off, I reach for her, and the absence of her body next to mine wakes me.

I have been trying to control my panic since the moment she got out of the car—telling myself that she is right, that our lives are too different, that I am not right for her—but the longer I go without hearing her voice, the less I feel in control. How could she just walk out? We could have discussed and worked everything out, and she just left. She stood there in that red dress, the wind blowing her hair across her tear-stained face, and I felt my heart break open.

How was I supposed to tell her in that moment that I loved her? We needed a plan, answers, and all I had to give her were the words. I didn't think they would be enough. But with every hour that passes, I am beginning to doubt every decision I've made. I sit down in a chair in my empty living room, my head in my hands, and there is a knock on the door. A jolt of hope slices through my chest, but as the door opens I realize it's just my dad. I completely forgot that he called earlier and said he'd be over after finishing up another day with the project in LA.

"Hey, Jess," he says, and the nickname is a wound in my side.

"Hey, Dad," I murmur, hugging him briefly. "Good to see you. Can I get you anything?"

"No, no. I just wanted to come by for a few hours before I fly out."

He sits in an armchair across from me, peering at me over the rims of his glasses.

"What's wrong?"

"Nothing. It's nothing you need to worry about. I can handle it."

"Jesse."

His voice tells me he knows I am lying. This is the man who taught me firsthand about the treacheries of love and he has never been wrong about gauging my moods. My mother wouldn't know the difference if I were upset or happy, wouldn't care to tell.

"It's Savannah," I say quietly, and then the story is coming out, piece by piece, and my dad rests his elbows on his knees and listens. I never share my emotions this way, but this is Savannah and somehow she makes everything different.

When I get to our fight, my dad stops me.

"Let me ask you something," he says. "When she said she was leaving, what did you say?"

"I don't remember. I was in shock. Everything happened so fast. One minute we were having a conversation and the next she was getting out of the car."

"Do you love her?"

I stare at him, then down at my hands.

"I don't know."

"Look, Jesse, if you can't even admit it to me you sure as hell won't be able to say it to her. Why is it so hard for you to accept?"

"Because life doesn't work that way. I can't just drop everything and leave with her. I can't be who she wants me to be."

"Who the hell is she asking you to be? She asked you to compromise, Jesse. She asked you to work with her and you didn't give an inch."

I feel a cold chill spreading inside me. He is saying all the things that deep down I know are true but haven't been able to bring myself to face.

"I know you saw a lot happen between your mother and I, Jesse," says my dad. He is looking at me earnestly, leaning forward in his chair, his elbows still resting on his bony knees. "But I don't want you thinking that love is something to avoid because of what happened when you were a child."

"It doesn't matter," I say coldly, hearing the ice

in my own voice. It reminds me of my mother, and in that moment I hate myself.

"Of course it does. Jesse, all you had to do is give Savannah one thing, and it's nothing you've offered to her. She just wants you."

I shake my head. Everything is so mixed up, my mind has been in a haze of pain since she left.

"I can't."

"Then you'll lose her. It's a choice you're going to have to make. It's simple. You love her. She loves you. It's only as complicated as you make it."

He drops the subject, and we talk about other things for a few hours until he leaves. I hug him goodbye, beyond words, and my dad thumps my back.

"Love you, son," he says. "I hope you choose what matters most to you." He claps my shoulder and walks to his car and I watch him go.

My parents are so completely different; it strikes me every time I see either of them. And look at Savannah and me—also very different from one another. How can we make this work? I run my hands through my hair, torn in a million directions. But the fact of the matter is staring me right in the face. I shut my front door behind me and hit the sand running.

I have done nothing but alternate between swimming and lying in bed since I walked home in the red dress. Swimming works the edge off my frustration and wears me out since I've been finding it impossible to sleep since we've been apart. Everything looks different: the sky is grayer, the air colder. The entire world seems empty of promise, hopeless. Paige and Sophie have been supportive, but I just shrug them off. I'm not ready to face their sympathy. I feel like such a fool. I thought if I gave him everything, he would meet me halfway. I thought if I loved him with everything I had, he would know how to love me back. I was wrong. But I don't doubt that I did the right thing by getting out of that car. I can't be with someone who takes everything from me, who holds my heart in his hands, who can't value that more than anything else. Maybe it's a steep price, but I can't believe it was too much to ask him to love me back, to give me himself in return. My chest aches, but I've cried out all my tears. Now I'm empty.

I hear footsteps coming down the hallway and I know it's Paige or Sophie with more soup.

"I don't want it, guys," I call shakily. "Please just leave me alone."

"You don't mean that."

The low husky voice makes my heart flip sideways in my chest. I peek out from the blankets on my bed, sure that I must be mistaken, that I'm dreaming. But I look up and he's there, standing over me, tall and perfect and everything. In that one second, everything is okay. But then I fall back to reality and remember that night and my brief bubble of happiness evaporates in my chest.

"What do you want, Jesse?" I whisper. Just having

him close is agonizing. I sit up and wrap myself in a blanket.

"Can I sit?" He gestures to my bed, and I shrug. He sits, piercing my heart with his turquoise eyes that I love so much. He takes my hand in his and I can barely stand the pain and pleasure of his touch.

"Savannah," he begins. "This past week has been agony. I wanted to pretend that I could live that way, that I could be okay again with all the things that used to matter to me before you."

I am frozen, locked into immobility by his words, but I refuse to allow myself to hope.

"You're right," he says quietly. "You were right about everything. I put more value on my career than our relationship, thinking I could work you around what I wanted to do. But you changed everything. It's not enough anymore. It doesn't matter to me in the same way. Everything has changed, since you."

I cannot believe what I am hearing. I am incapable of movement or speech, but I feel my insides warming as though I am finally escaping the freeze that has enveloped me since I left him. He looks concerned, taking my other hand and searching my eyes with his. It is heaven to have him here, just to have him close enough to touch, but I am not ready to speak yet.

"Please," Jesse says. "I'm so sorry. You gave me all you had and I gave you parts of me. I held back, thinking it would be better, more reasonable. I refused to admit that my world has shifted so that you're at the center."

He runs his hand through his hair.

"I still care about my career," he says. "But it's not even comparable to the way I feel about you. I'm willing to meet you halfway, Savannah. More than halfway. You matter to me more than I know how to say. You're everything."

This, this is what I've wished for since the first time Jesse made love to me. All I needed were the words, the knowledge that he felt the same way, that he would love me the way I loved him without reservation and without limit. He takes my face in his, running his thumbs over my cheekbones, gently touching my swollen eyes, and then his lips are on mine and I can barely stand the heat that immediately rises between us.

"Jess," I say, and I feel his lips curve against mine.

"I thought I'd never hear you say my name like that again," he breathes, and then we are in each other's arms and his hands are caressing my face and sliding down my back and all too soon I lose my breath and lay my head on his chest.

"Savannah," he murmurs, his hands moving over me. "I love you."

I look up into his piercing eyes, linking his fingers with mine. "I love you, too," I say. He runs his thumb over my lower lip, gently tugging, and then pulls me close, and then words are no longer necessary. His touch warms my skin and awakens my body as we slowly undress each other without rush, without hurry. Everything is magnified, with the knowledge of his feelings for me making every touch more intense. When the light floods in through the window, it fills his eyes with light. I could spend forever touching every inch of his skin, learning him all over again. He skims his lips over my neck where my pulse pounds, and I lose track of everything but what he brings to me.

"Look at me, baby," he says as he slides inside me, filling me, and my eyes flutter open. He's finally seeing me for who I am, loving me for who I am. I press my lips to his and give him all of me willingly, without reservation, knowing I have all of him in return.

Afterwards, when he holds me, I can feel his heart pounding in his chest, the beat matching mine, and within that rhythm, I can hear the promise of forever.

THE END